T0354927

Never Knew

Order this book online at www.trafford.com
or email orders@trafford.com

Most Trafford titles are also available at major online book retailers.

Print information available on the last page.

ISBN: 978-1-4120-9874-8 (sc)
ISBN: 978-1-4251-4212-4 (hc)

Trafford rev. 07/04/2018

North America & international
toll-free: 1 888 232 4444 (USA & Canada)
fax: 812 355 4082

Never Knew

Tiesa Turan

To my blue eyed sun shiny angel

Who simply entered my life

Unaware of the emotional swirl headed my way

You took my hand, whispering softly

Don't be afraid, come along

Leading me out from the shadows

Spreading my wings open to the horizons

Learn, except, know and grow

But most of all to fly high, high as I possibly can

With my deepest appreciation, love and gratitude,

I dedicate this to you

With all my love,

I thank you.

Table of Contents

UNTIL NEXT TIME

I WANT YOU TO touch me, every part of me – feel me – know me.

Cup my face and kiss me softly, trace my lips with your tongue. Caress my hair and look deep into my eyes, then kiss me with wild abandonment, like you've visualized this moment, this chance to be together.

Slowly making a trail down my neck, your lips leave their mark. As your hands find my breasts, your fingers playfully tug at my nipples, arousing them to a peak. Your warm mouth covers a nipple and my body shivers with emotion. I moan with pleasure as you suck on me, teasing me. You cup my other tit and taunt my nipple with your finger.

I run my hands through your hair and guide your head down, past my belly and as you are lowering yourself, your body slithers over mine and I'm swept up with such a desire to have you. All the while your lips rove over me finding their way between my legs. You nip at my hair, licking the inside of my thighs, while your finger slides in and out of me, ever so slowly.

Before I let you go any further, I take your hand in mine and suck on your finger tasting myself and reminding you with my tongue how I'll be pleasuring you. Without hesitation your mouth covers my pussy, so warm and wet. As you bring me to a climax my whole being comes alive like a burning fire. I reach for your head and bring your face to mine, kissing you – tasting you. Running my fingernails through the hair on your chest, my hand reaches down for your dick. Rubbing it, up and down, exciting your senses, the hardness feels so good in my palm.

Without speaking, you roll onto your back and I settle myself in between your open legs. I glide my lips down to your sweet flesh, licking the tip, covering your head with my mouth, tasting you. Tantalizing you with my tongue, I slowly take all of you in. Sucking on you makes me tingly inside – moving upwards – teasing, then downwards – so pleasing. Can you feel the warmth of my mouth as my lips slide up and down your cock?

Your hands in my hair, holding my head, guiding my movements, we fall into rhythm. I hear you moan, whispering how good it feels. My nails gingerly slide over your stomach, down your legs, creating a swell of sensations inside you and almost, bringing you to the brink of ecstasy.

You pull me towards you and I straddle myself over you, placing your dick inside of me. Moving in unison, focused with a burning desire, feeling each other mentally, stroking one another physically – our bodies fitting like a glove. You place your hands on my hips, guiding me, moving me, letting us drift away to the motion. Gently you pull me towards you so my chest lays slightly on yours as our bodies rub against each other, my nipples erect to hardness.

We intertwine our legs and roll over, as you look down at me, you take my hands in yours and clasp them together, in a strong hold. Staring into the depths of one another, our bodies joined, matching each other move for move, bringing ourselves to the edge and finally... letting the world slip away, into oblivion.

NEVER THE END

I'VE BECOME SO WET for you even though you're far away. I drip with the thoughts of being able to fuck you again. I'm in need of it so much that my body quivers as I visualize the moments. Memory plays your voice inside my head, hearing the deepness – the sexiness of it and my world goes wild.

We begin kissing with such fervor that makes my senses come alive. Our tongues do a dance, tasting – exploring. I run my fingers through your hair and moan with pleasure, you make me so hot and crazy with your tongue and lips. Before I know it, that luscious tongue of yours finds its way to my juicy little pussy. Every move your making, I take it all in – sucking on my clit, licking me all over, up and down until I become numb – inside and out! Your finger glides in and out of my pussy, tracing its way to my ass, teasing and pleasing me. Gently you slide the tip of your finger into my wet ass. Sucking on my pussy and fingering my ass, you give my body so many emotions that I'm feeling dizzy, but Oh so high! I moan in pleasure and arch my back so you know of the rush you're giving me. I'm feeling the need to be fucked, hard – fast furious, but softly – slowly and gently. The way only you know how.

You bring me to orgasm so easily and so many times. I am so wet, all over; it doesn't seem to want to stop. You bring out such a passion in me that I've only been able to dream about until now, now it is reality. Slowly you move up my body, inching yourself to my mouth, releasing onto my lips and open mouth the sweetness of orgasm I've poured out to you. The flavor is pure sex, pure cum, you – mixed with me.

Opening my legs wide and straddling over me, your throbbing cock slides into my cunt; I am so ready for you. The ecstasy is unbelievable, your dick fits just right – fucking me the way I like, the way I need it. Giving me enough to keep me sedated, you turn me onto my side, guiding my head to your hardness, my lips, my mouth – cover you. Oh, how I love sucking on your manhood. Your hand wrapped around your dick, turns me on.

Tormenting you with my tongue, tracing the outline of your rim, sucking your head, then with one swift move – I put all of you inside. Sucking up and down, licking your shaft, down to your balls, then up again until the moisture in my mouth – wet as my pussy, runs down your stiff, pulsating cock. As I'm into a rhythm, pleasuring you, your hands are a frenzy of movements – playing with me, caressing my nipples, rubbing my pussy, teasing my ass with the length of your finger until my whole being is screaming inside! Knowing and sensing what I need, you place me on my belly, anticipating your entrance, suddenly a sear of fire rushes up my spine – goose bumps scatter all over my back. Feeling you inside me, fucking my ass, giving me such a sensation, all I can think of is MORE; give it to me – all of it – all of you!

You place you're strong hands around my waist, thrust after hungry thrust, my ass gets wetter and hornier. Your fingers run through my hair and you grab a handful – holding onto it, pulling it gently towards you. Then you start rubbing my back with your other hand and chase the goose bumps away. Your hands glide around my hips – thighs, spreading my cheeks apart as your dick slides in and out of my ass.

Knowing you're watching focused with a hungry desire to please, my knees grow weak, drawing a shaky half sobbing breath you take me over the edge. With every move you make, I follow. Changing positions, never missing a beat, we're into a rhythm, caught up in the exhilarating tide of emotions; your cock slides into my wet pussy. I whisper how you fuck me so intensely, only you, you make me feel so damn good! Your dick feels so right in my little pussy.

Holding your body close to mine, I can feel your balls rub against my ass, driving me even crazier. I hear your voice – talking dirty to me, turning me on like I've never been before. I'm so tuned into everything sexually and turned on by you, that the link between thoughts and words are instantaneous. Scream for me – fuck me – scream for me and fill my senses with the extremity of your orgasm, take me with you to the heights you'll achieve. Fuck me until we can't see straight, where there is just a plateau of wild and far away places with total abandonment, which we never want to come down from... traveling through land that is not forbidden.

The gust of your climax is the most gratifying, but yet tranquil thing I've ever experienced, the force of it is almost too much to consume. The release is so powerful, it is like nothing I've ever felt before and every time the journey is such a way I've never traveled and so much more than my mind can conceive. As we lay there surrounded by the air of pleasure we've given to each other, the power of sexual communication is stronger than any words ever spoken.

LONG WAY DOWN

THE WAY YOU SUCK on me sends waves of pleasure through me. Your warm mouth and hot tongue cover me so well – every inch of my juice box. You suck on my clit and nip at it gently with your teeth as your tongue slides in and out of my wet pussy hole.

Relaxing my body, my thoughts turn to you and I focus mentally on every touch and every stroke you give to me. All I feel is how you suck on me like a delicious treat. Your hands reaching up to my nipples, with your fingertips you tease and twirl them. You seduce me into a flaming orgasm.

Suddenly you start licking my ass – going down, coming up, and making a trail from my pussy to my ass. Driving me in deeper, I cannot tell which is wetter. Slowly you start rubbing oil over my entire body, around my tits, down my belly, not missing any curves, dripping oil onto my pussy, hesitating there to smooth it in, fingering me, teasing me, leaving me with shameless want.

As your hands explored all over my body, I followed them with my own. Caressing my tits, playing with my nipples – rubbing myself, making a trail to my pussy, that you've already made so wanton and ready for pleasure. Rubbing my clit back and forth as my other hand tugs at a nipple, I realize you are no longer touching me.

Stroking myself now, I ease a finger into my juicy pussy, so wet and so soft, all the while my palm is rubbing against my clit. I slide my finger out to suck on it, tasting and savoring. The silkiness of oil is shinning all over my body mixed with the sweet scent of cum, filling the air.

Knowing that you are watching me intently, burning blue eyes following every stroke, turns me on even more because I know I'm giving you a thrill as I please myself. You arouse my sexuality by letting me be free, leaving me to explore.

Slowly I slide a finger into my wet ass, the pleasure of the entrance reminds me of how your stiff hard cock feels in there. Having a finger in my pussy with another up my ass and the measured pace of palm on clit, I lose myself to pure self-pleasure, with thoughts of you – us, fucking and sucking spinning round and round in my head.

Suddenly your hands cover my body, grabbing my thighs, rubbing my hips, and feeling your dick pushing its way inside of me. "'Oh, you are so hard, ready to penetrate, to pulsate inside my wet juicy little pussy, fucking me so good!"

My hands grab a hold of your ass and push you deeper, filling me up until I'm completely swept away. Moving with lithe grace, you slip your cock into my ass, from pussy to ass, they're both so wet and always ready for you. With every thrust up my ass we fall into a primal dance, thoughts fade to the background, emotions exploding, our mentality blurs easily into a mass of energy, growing stronger and getting caught by the hunger of our sexual appetite. Fucking until we see stars – reaching our destination, we simultaneously erupt…

falling…

falling…

fading away…

TAKING MY
CHANCES

TODAY MUST BE MY lucky day! Walking in the door after an early morning rain, there you were, calling on the phone. What are you doing, led to, I'll see you in a while. All I thought about on my drive to meet you was how I could please you – the way you like.

Before getting into the shower, halfway undressed, you pulled me towards you and just ravaged me – kissing me, rubbing my tits, then taking one in your hand to suck on my nipple, bringing it to a peak, stroking my pussy through my jeans – every movement making me hotter and crazier! Sensing in one another that we were both in need, the need to have each other, we kissed with such a passion until our knees went weak with endless desire.

As we were getting into the shower, I told you exactly what I wanted to do to you. How I wanted to, "Lick you – suck you and finger fuck you. To suck on your balls and follow the line down to your ass, then up to suck on your big dick."

Slipping out of the shower, into the bed, we touched each other like we've never before – fueled with intense emotion. Turning you on your stomach, I started rubbing oil on your back and proceeded to rub myself all over you – gliding my tits down your back, over your ass while my nails traced down every inch my plump round tits left behind. Spreading your cheeks apart, I kiss and suckle one side of your ass at a time. Then I lick your ass-hole, circling the outside with my tongue and getting into a groove of licking and sucking, up and down, down to your balls, back up and around your hole – licking side to side, my tongue darts in and out of your ass-hole. I can feel it getting wet as moisture begins to seep out, just as mine does when you do what you do to me! It was a pleasure to hear your deep voice moaning, letting me know you liked it.

I take a finger and rub it up and down your ass feeling the moisture inside your hole and what my tongue has created. Making sure you are ready and wet enough, I run my tongue over your ass again, feeling it, sucking it, and licking you with such delight that you spin into a new sun rise. I ask you to rise up onto your knees; slowly I ease a finger into your ass, inch – by – inch, sliding it further… deeper.

Lying on my back, I push myself forward and lower my head to suck on your huge cock. Sucking on your dick as I finger your ass, just playing with you this way is like a raging river. Being in control gives me the freedom to satisfy you as much as you do me.

Caught up in my desire to fuck you, I feel you wrapping your arms around my legs and waist, pulling me towards you a bit. You start rubbing me all over with oil, fingering my pussy and then fingering my ass-hole. As you do I try to match my rhythm to yours, the way you are fingering my ass, so we can be in tune and ride the wave together as it gently consumes you… and I. Sucking, licking and fingering each other, so much want, so much need.

Lying down on your back, your cock is so hard, thrusting straight up, "Slide it in your ass," I hear you say. Sitting on top of you with your dick gliding up my ass, is pure pleasure. In and out, up and down, lost is the ground beneath my feet, losing myself to the motion, with your strong hands around my waist, matching each other perfectly. I love it when your dick is up my ass, fucking me so good, talking dirty to each other, your hard cock in my ass – fucks me just right. "You love getting your ass fucked… yeah… I do… love the way you fuck it."

Drifting away, closing my eyes, I surrender to you completely, let me fuck your dick, fucking you feels so right – suck my nipples – oh yeah, that's so good. Stroke after stroke, we're in so deep – loss of time, lost to everything… you explode inside me – releasing all the energy of yourself into me. The orgasm is so extreme I'm overcome by the swell you've created, breathing has no purpose, swirling away with you – holding on tight – into the depths of our wild uncharted journey.

Realizing that reality is upon us once again, we notice how the sun is shining so brilliantly in the afternoon sky.

THE QUICK FIX

KNOWING I WOULDN'T BE seeing you, my weekend was okay. Heavy into thought, tormenting my mind, body, soul and self. As I was thinking, my pussy was dripping, becoming so moist with want for you. I imagined the way you stir me up with those taunting hands always knowing where to touch – what to fondle – when I need my ass smacked and those questing lips that know how to suck and lick every inch of me. I start reeling from the way my mind has run rampant.

So on Monday, I began to wander, if I call you and throw some tasty lines your way, maybe you would bite? I dressed with out a bra or underwear, preparing myself for a yes. Well, you took the bait and met me.

We parked in the woods on that sun-shiny day and made small conversation. I interrupted with a single-minded notion that, "I really wanted to get laid!" I was sure that, no longer could I keep my distance from you, the restraint to not have you – now – inside me, was overwhelming.

Making ourselves comfortable in the back seat of your truck, you ran your hand up my bare leg under my skirt; your finger, quickly slides into my soft wetness – making me burn for you. Oh how it feels so damn good. Pulling my legs down, you bury your face in my hot pussy, taking the moment in, intently watching you with awe, your lips suckle mine – I get off so easily, the way a lightening bolt streaks against the sky.

Changing my scenery, discarding my skirt, you sit up so I can put your hard cock in my mouth, which rose so tall when you were drinking in my juices. Your hand covers my head, guiding me towards you, I close my eyes on the way down, as your dick fills my mouth and open them to focus on the way up, up … and then back down again, licking you around your rim, flicking at your slit, my mouth becomes so wet because I finally have you inside me – your big dick pulsating on my tongue. It doesn't matter where or which hole you're in or what kind of high I get from it all, it's the different kind of rushes that blaze through me whenever you are there.

Overheated with desire, you lay me down and take me, breathing in the scent of man – of you, I suck, kiss and lick your chest as you fuck me – fuck my pussy, it's so hot and wet.

Rearranging our positions, I sit on top of you now, taking myself on a heady ride. My chest is in your face, you suck on my tits – one at a time, pushing them together to suck on them at once, triggering every nerve ending inside me to reach higher – farther, spilling over and beyond, my quivering fingers run through your hair until the current forces me to achieve, climax and magically melt away.

Turning me over so I'm kneeling on the seat, you get behind me and insert your throbbing hardness into my wet ass. Gripping the seat with one hand – kneading the softness, I reach down to rub my clit as your probing cock fucks my ass, feeling you lifting my cheeks up a bit so you can watch, I begin to gnaw on the top of the seat.

Steady and certain, again you tear at my senses until we are both consumed – just letting go. Fulfilling our quest with one last, great burst, our uninhibited spirits break loose, soaring far away, as we sway … swirl and descend from the ultimate release.

NO ONE LIKE YOU

YOU LAID ME DOWN across the table, as you sat on the bench, your mouth is level with my pussy. You start pushing back and forth with your feet and the glider picks up the pace and motion, gliding back and forth as you start sucking on my juice box, I feel the swaying begin to take over my senses.

I open my eyes and as I'm lost on this journey, I see the palm trees fraying upon the breeze, their movement is like mine – gently stirring to the rhythm you've created inside me. I feel as though I'm one of the palms, floating back and forth as your tongue licks me up and down, darting in and out of my wet pussy – the sight of the stars up above look near enough that I find myself reaching out, as if to pluck one from the sky, but I grasp onto you, to enclose your head in my hand – to run my fingers through your soft hair.

Sensuously feeling your cheeks as your mouth dives deeper into my ocean of silkiness, my hot juices flowing inside you – all around your tongue, drinking in the taste of my sweetness. The sound of our passionate, intimate escape triggers me back to the gliding and I hear myself softly murmuring to you. Suspended in time between the earth and sky, safe in our solitude, I feel as though I'm on the breeze being swept away by you.

No longer able to bear the need that has crept deep down inside, I sit up and guide you backwards so I can ease my softness onto your hardness. Straddling you on the bench, your hot breath caresses my tits; cupping your face I kiss your lips gently – deeply – madly, tasting my warm juices all over your mouth. You trail your lips down my neck and the wind rustles the palms, sending shivers down my spine, but I feel the heat and warmth enclose around my nipple, tracing the outline, tugging with your lips – I can't help but lose myself to the feeling of it all. As my head tilts backward, you take advantage of my nipples, tight and taunt – peaking up and out, circling them rhythmatically, pleasuring me the way only you know how to.

Taking me beyond and far away to places I can only travel with you and through you. Melting into you and the ecstasy you pour out of yourself is like a breaking wave, rolling and churning me, drowning and overpowering me with the intensity of every emotion threatening to overtake me. Words can never describe the sensational havoc that courses through my veins and body. Feeling as though you're lifting my soul – freeing it, to explore the depths and realms of lovemaking.

Since you know my body, inside and out, I relax in your presence and give myself to you with a self-satisfied tranquility. Your hands touch me expertly, playing and teasing, making me dizzy like they always do. I love fucking you – love to be fucked by you – your dick feels so hard in my pussy and I'm dripping so much around your cock, making it slippery. I ride you and grind you as you suck on my nipples – one at a time, back and forth – driving me to a frenzy, your hand comes down upon my ass cheek, Oh baby, you don't know how much that makes me crazy and then ... again – you smack the other side. I want you so bad, I can feel every inch of your cock pulsate and grow harder inside me after every single smack, it makes me wetter and hornier until a gratifying warmth runs through me and I'm just so lost to all but you.

Combining the fucking I'm getting – the sucking your lips have accustomed themselves to and the smacking on my cheeks, I grab a hold of the bench, arch my back and let it all happen. Shuddering and igniting with a scream of passion, I start to feel your explosion of fireworks bursting inside me, as my hot juices collide against yours – the freedom of it engulfs us completely, breathing out so I can breathe you in – together we glide on, huddled close, carrying each other to the uppermost point of our sexual union.

HOLD ONTO ME

WE MET IN THE morning, on a rainy day at the shore; I thought it was a perfect day to lie next to you, wrapped up in your masculine arms. We lay on the couch touching each other – familiarizing our hands with the smoothness of our skin. My fingers trailed their way down your sweet smelling, soft nakedness.

Fondling your dick, I inched my mouth down the side of your chest, towards your belly – still holding your dick, I take your head and slowly run my lips across it, flicking my tongue inside your hole, my mouth covers you completely and I start sucking on you with so much desire and pleasure inside of me; ready to burst out that I feel you growing, harder and stronger on my warm tongue. The juices in my mouth begin to flow as I place all of your stiffness into my wet mouth, then licking you up and down, down one side – up again, pausing to suck on your head and then down over the other side. I've got such a good rhythm going on that I'm wrapped up and losing my conscious self along the way. I love sucking on your cock, making it rise and throb in my warm, mouth. Just the way it feels when you're inside my wet, welcoming pussy. I can actually feel your dick fucking my cunt, as my mouth sucks and fucks your cock.

You reach down to feel the moisture dripping between my legs, to rub it all around me. You run your fingers over my clit and one slips inside. "Ohh baby, you just know exactly how and when to get me shaken again." Sucking on your dick gets me so high and now you're sliding finger – slippery wet – goes back and forth, driving me to the edge once again. "I am ready for anything you're willing to give me, anywhere you want to stick it, do me as you will – I AM YOURS!'"

In a heated rush your face goes between my legs, tasting my sweet juicy little pussy, getting your lips and mouth so very wet. Dreaming of those luscious lips I love to suck on after you've drank of me. I lay myself sideways so you can finger fuck me, gently your strong hand guides my head to your cock and at the same time we begin sucking on each other. Memorizing the softness and hardness, our mouths devour and savor the taste of you... and me. I want you so bad; I want to be fucked so good!

Sensing my wantonness, you change our positions, as your kneeling on the floor, I slide my ass towards the edge of the couch and you give my pussy such a fucking that it takes me beyond any existence ever. You are so damn good. My hands caress my own body and I feel your eyes upon me, you were watching me, I knew. Silently I take myself to another level; my world became the world of exploration. Your gaze burns through me, all around – up and down – every inch of me, resting upon my face to glide along with me as my facial expressions speak to you through slightly closed eyes and parted lips. You read my bodies reaction like a book.

Wild and willing – I arch my back so you can penetrate me deeper and harder, scratching along the fabric, kneading my nails gingerly into my shoulders, as a kitten does when purring – you fuck my pussy so good, making it so wet and juicy, I'm your little cunt. I get such a good one when your cock is grinding inside so nice and slow, but hard and thrusting.

After a while you guide my head, wrapping your fingers through my hair, to suck on your dick – bringing forth the wetness into my mouth. You move yourself in to the chair, in front of the windows over looking the ocean, as you are there, I sit on the floor facing you and trace my body with oil, and the scent fills the air, playing with your senses. I cover myself and enjoy every moment of touching my body – in front of you. Slowly moving with sensuality – the sexual heat radiates from my body, flowing into yours. If only you knew my thoughts, the visions running across my mind so bright and vibrant. I'm aware of you so much that I get a thrill just knowing you are here, in front of me, observing it all – watching me rub oil over my body, touching my tits, rubbing my pussy.

Stroke after stroke my finger glides in and out of my juicy pussy, as you watch, I slowly slip another finger into my ass and you tell me that everywhere my fingers go, you envision your cock there. My juices start flowing from my pussy down to my ass and I begin to feel electrified because I know I'll be getting it there soon – because you give it to me everywhere so fucking good.

Deeply into pleasuring myself, you slowly inch me onto the chair telling me not to stop what I'm doing, while you place me in it – your beautiful, hot mouth consumes my pussy, licking up the wetness, sucking in my juices, going down on me the way I do you. You place a finger inside me, caught up in this wave – you place another just slightly inside my ass, doing me with such an intense desire to please, you finger fuck my pussy and ass in such a way that I can't stop releasing every bit of juice all over your fingers. You know I need it now, I want that hard cock of yours in my ass, to glide in and out of my holes – whichever one you feel needs it more.

As your dick inches into my wet and ready ass, I lose myself again to you, to something odd and unexplainable, trust and gratification warmly trace a way throughout my body as I wander in blind faith, the blissfulness of pleasure and pain! I place my legs up on your chest with my feet resting on your shoulders; your hands reach down to hold onto my arms. Seeing you kneeling there, watching your crystal blue eyes sparkle like prisms, the emotions write themselves across your face.

Every part of you, I'm aware of – I thrive on every move you make upon me. Time stands still... hanging in a hazy moment, the waves on this sea of joy still roll in; with every splash my entire body engulfs itself with goose bumps. "Holy Shit, what a fucking rush you have swirled around me!" I run my hands up and down my legs, across my belly, chasing the goose bumps down my arms and over my chest. Comprehending the tide of ecstasy that swept around me, that you pull from deep inside me is overwhelming – you fuck me so fucking good. I hear myself saying, "Don't stop – please don't stop – fuck me, give it to me, Oh baby – your cock feels so nice up my ass."

Drifting on the wind, I escalate and hold on for the ride, spilling over into you, my body grows numb – realizing the loss of all control, I feel as though I am not really in my body, I am so gone to the world around me. You can take me any time through the rolling mist, a million miles away, lost within the depths of the deep blue.

MISSION
ACCOMPLISHED

THINKING OF YOU WHILE I was laying out all day, feeling the sun caress my skin with it's warmth, just the way you seem to touch me all over – not only physically but mentally. I called to ask if your offer still stands. I should have known your answer and I knew I wasn't going to turn you down.

As we drive around, you take me past the places I've seen before. I think to myself – you say all the right things at exactly the right time; you are whom I've always dreamed of. If you can only give me this little time together, than it is more than enough – than you could imagine.

Even as we're conversing every thing seems to be turning sexual – the deepness of your voice, the way my eyes begin to look over you and the way my laughter comforts your ears. Noticing the radiant sun in the afternoon sky as the music plays on and the scent of your manly body drifts to my nose. I try to behave myself for as long as I can but ya know, I just licked my lips and can't keep my eyes off your dick – I'm getting wet and I can see you growing hard.

You notice the glazed look on my face and edge your cock out of your button fly and ask, "Is this what you want?" Now that your flesh is in full view, there is no turning back. Going down on you while you drive is the coolest thing. I wrap my lips around you and just suck you and lick your dick as I would the sweetest piece of candy my mouth has ever tasted. Not responding to your questions because I am otherwise indulged and into sucking on your huge cock – I shake my head yes – you should know once I get a hold of your hardness my pussy starts to drip. I feel your hand reach down to grab my ass and I wrap an arm around the back of your seat just to have something to hold on to.

While you're driving, I keep the same motion as your vehicle – if your foot is heavy on the pedal and we're cruising, than I'm sucking on you, up and down – fast and then faster, as you let off the gas I slow down, to suck on your head gently, lick around your rim, round and round – over your hole with faintness and contentment until my mouth begins to water. I know you want me as much as I do you because your dick is so erect and hard in my mouth.

I feel you pulling over – lifting my eyes to see our destination, I raise up my head and catch a glimpse of the setting sun. Turning to face you – you read the look of hunger in my eyes and start undressing, following your lead, I do the same.

While you're in the drivers' seat, I straddle myself over top of you and I hear your husky, whispered words, flowing into my ears. As we start fucking, I realize that we're on the side of the road, parked along the forest with an open field on the other side. Our bodies joined together moving to the beat that burns inside our souls. Heightened by the knowledge that at any time, some one could drive by – you let me know you've got the front covered and I let you know that I've got the back covered and so with that little exchange, it gets me off just a bit more.

It's a mixed adrenaline rush – a different kind of high, but the satisfaction you are giving me is unbelievable – you take me to the edge and over ... over again, until finally what I'm feeling can't be kept inside and I start whispering my sweet words, "You make my pussy so wet, you fuck my pussy so good, I cum so easily all over your hard, throbbing, pulsating cock that slides in and out of my warmth.'"

Cradling your head as I speak – your strong hands grip my waist and push down while your dick plunges deeper in me, up and down our bodies gently move and I feel you so completely submerged inside me. Trying to keep my eyes focused on the road behind, my being only feels one thing and sends its signals to my mind that begins to run rampant. I slightly close my eyes as my words float through the air ... taking us both along the breeze, like a swallow borne on the wind – only to realize that not a single soul has gone by while we fulfilled our horny cravings and sexual desires.

GOT TO HAVE YOU

MY THOUGHTS WERE ON you yesterday – hitting the wall at 180, when the white flag comes up – sort of similar to the way we fuck each other, as our hearts pound rapidly along with our maddening inflamed arousal. So I called to see if you were still alive and the only comfort I got was to hear your voice on the machine. I began to think of how you do me so good – memories are a beautiful thing.

Anyhow, my day led to be a very peaceful one, I went out and made myself comfortable in the sunshine. As I lay there, I started to rub lotion on my body and my mind took a journey – my hands began to turn into yours – I rubbed myself so nicely and saw your fingers instead of mine, trailing their prints down my belly – circling around, the way a plane does before landing at its destination. The breeze picks up and flows through my hair, teasing my senses, as your finger has been gliding in and out of my hot -n- juicy pussy ... so gently and calmly.

Coming in for touch down, I snap out of the spell I've placed on myself and reach for my drink. While it wets my lips, the coolness seeps out of your lips and onto my clit and sends shivers through my body. Now I can see the top of your head between my thighs – I feel your tongue, mouth – licking and sucking, sliding in and out of my soft wet pussy. I reach out to run my fingers through your hair. God ... you suck on me so damn good! Sitting in the sun, with my pussy hanging out, I can't stop thinking of you and how good you do me.

The wind seemingly knows my thoughts, picks me up and carries me away. Somehow I feel you on that summer breeze, drifting through my body – touching the very heart of me – leading me on to follow – down the roads you choose. Going down, down farther, I start to suck on your hard cock that's always ready for a good sucking because you know my tongue, itching to travel the throbbing, beating path of your dick.

I begin to feel the moisture in my mouth building up – I take your head with my lips, not touching your sun-tanned chest or any other part of you with my hands – only my soft lips connected to your smooth head. I run my tongue down your shaft and bring you back up with my lips, taking your head and gently sucking it into my mouth. I begin to suck on you – wrapping a hand around your cock, thrusting you down my throat.

I get wet all over – I love to suck on you and fuck your dick with my mouth. I memorize the softness of your head, the curve of your rim, the way your hole feels – I enjoy diving in and out of it, mmm ... the way I suck on your ass – darting in and around your hole – man, you give me such control, it's so fucking awesome! My mind creates the image and my body relives the sensations. You see these are my thoughts, which tumble through my head.

I take a glimpse at the outer world, but only for a minute and then I return back to touching your balls, I look at your mound of hair, noticing the color, remembering how your balls feel in the palm of my hand and the softness on my fingertips. I suck on your dick the way I do because no one ever let me suck it and really get into it the way you let me, it's definitely always an adventure when my mouth gets on a roll – my tongue making you crazy – my moisture dripping from my lips. I know the best is yet to come, but still I give you all that I got. I really can never get enough of you – your dick so big and hard in my mouth, you fit just right, you know I could suck on you 'til tomorrow.

Realizing I've been daydreaming in the sun and its rays have sunk into my body, I feel as if you and I just fucked. I reach down to feel the moisture between my legs – just by the thoughts of you that ran through my mind and your seducing ways, made me horny and the heat that is radiating off my pussy reminds me of the warmth that is created by you when you are bumping and grinding inside my cunt. Weaving my thoughts to how you feel when you are inside me. Your cock fucks my juicy little cunt, oh so good – man, how you fuck me, you drive me crazy – take me to places far, far away from here. I should be your diamond girl because I fit perfectly on your dick.

Sometimes the fantasy is so real – you actually blow my mind, I need to pinch myself and get a hold of my bearings. Fucking me here, doing me there – positions always changing, different currents running through my veins. Never the same place nor the same way, but always the high heights – cruising through the valleys, drifting higher than the clouds, but still seeing beyond, above and below – such an awesome flight!

I wonder if you see what I see and imagine with me. I can never get enough, yet you seem to always sedate me. My mind carries me away, any which way the wind blows – on the most magical... mystical ride I can exceed to when you are not here to pleasure me. There are times when I need you like never before – can't you feel the change you've brought over me. There's this deep, locked up feeling inside and you – only you hold the key.

I LOVE YOU

I'M SO ASTOUNDED BY the way you make me feel. You offer me the freedom to experience so many different levels of pleasure. You opened the door with outstretched arms, welcoming me inside ... inside to a foreign land with an unknown tongue. Where my mind thinks the levels are not so safe, but my senses are intoxicated by the lure. Sometimes feeling as though I leaped from an imaginary cliff, falling through the air, a long and slow fall, with time a plenty to remember every sway and swoop. The way you touch me – the way you move me. I can't help but become so wet and horny.

I love to be with you on days like this, when it's misty and raining. Sitting in the hot tub, relaxing our bodies and minds, stroking each other, we drift closer together and start kissing so softly – your lips brush across mine, so smooth – gently savoring the taste of one another, drinking in the moment as your kisses satisfy my heart. I totally relax my body and enjoy the feel of your tongue caressing mine; the passion in your kisses is riveting, tender and caring. I feel your sexual power seeping into me. As we make love with our mouths, I reach down for your hardness, taking it in my hand I slowly rub you up and down – my thumb trails over your hole. Your mouth changes motion and you kiss me with such want, sucking on my tongue – sucking on my lower lip, the thrill is almost overbearing.

I feel you backing up, inching yourself to the corner and sitting up on the edge to get comfortable. I kneel a bit out of the water and stick my tongue out to slurp at the droplets of water on your chest. I lower my head to suck on your dick and now the journey begins. You know how I love to pleasure you; your cock in my mouth pacifies me like nothing ever could. I want you to enjoy this as much as I am going to.

While I'm sucking your nice hard cock, I move my pussy directly in front of a jet, as I lick you all over – I feel the hardness of you inside my mouth throbbing. The water is massaging my clit and since I have you in my mouth; I imagine you fucking me. My lips traveling all around, my tongue running up and down your shaft and the water pressure flirting with my pussy gets me off. The only thing my mind can feel is you inside my wet pussy and my body begins to tremble, even though you are really in my mouth and all of this craziness brings me to climax. I feel the moisture from my mouth all over your dick as if my mouth came also.

Making our way out of the water, you proceed to finger fuck me – in my pussy, into my ass – both at the same time. "Whoa … you're going to make me dizzy!" I bend over to position myself better and to give you total control. You give me so much to look forward to and I take all that you're willing to give to me now. I want your dick inside me so bad and knowing that I'll have it soon, I climax again – my knees grow weak and I collapse where I stand. Your chuckle of wicked amusement rolls out of your mouth as I hear you say, "You are such an easy little cunt – so easy to please."

Returning to my senses, I join you on the bed. I reach out for the oil and start rubbing it all over myself and a devilish smile creeps over my lips as I squirt some on your chest, I know what the scent of oil does to you. We rub the oil into and all over our bodies, touching ourselves – eyeing each other up. I move closer to you, reaching for your dick and begin to suck on it. I just can't stay away from it – it's the best toy I've ever had.

As I'm sucking on your cock, your hands start their journey

over my body – tweaking a nipple, fingers sliding into my wet pussy, spreading the juices to my ass, as I feel your finger slip into my hole. Every move you make, I'm aware of and I suck on you that much better; every sensation you give me I try to give one back to you.

You lay me on my stomach and go crazy with the oil. Spreading it all over my whole back, your strong hands smoothing it down my arms, trickling it over my ass – gently massaging my cheeks, moving down my legs, all the way to my feet, then back up again through the whole process until you are at my neck. You simply free yourself to the motion as your hands cover me completely and man… does it ever feel great. I am so relaxed now, I feel as though I am not in my body – hanging in a hazy moment – so peaceful, floating with the current of sensations you've created in me.

Ever so gently, I feel your hard cock enter me and now… the voyage has begun. I love to be fucked by you, you know everything about my body, when to tease me and exactly how to please me, you know me from my head to my toes! You'll be fucking me so good and then in the next minute, you're making total love to me. Fast with an urgency but then slowly with compassion and following you through these twists and turns makes me dizzy with emotion and I try to stay on course with you but you take me higher with every curve.

Suddenly, I surrender to you completely – a total breakdown occurs and from that point on I am yours for the taking and I know you can feel the change come over me. Fucking my pussy the way you do – feeling the heat inside is pure ecstasy. The friction from your hard cock just fucking me… fucking me and fucking me – my cunt gets soooo hot and then becomes soooo juicy! You turn me on like no one else – there is no one like you.

Lying on my stomach while you fucked my pussy and went for a ride, another trip begins to take its course because I feel you slowly sliding your cock up my asshole, sometimes I can't distinguish one from the other because they are both so wet. Being inside my ass, I am easily broken by the extreme tide of pleasure that rips through me, leaving me vulnerable – as your fucking it, Oh so good.

My pussy yearns for your touch and you – the expert lover that you are, reaches down under me and slides a finger up my pussy with soft caresses over my clit every now and again. Holy shit… that feels heavenly – bringing me to an amazing climax once again, as you do so often to me and for me, you are such a good man! My state of mind is oblivious to all but you.

Entering my wet, juicy pussy – giving me that wonderful cock of yours, thrusting inside – deeper and deeper, I reach behind me and slip my finger into my asshole. As I do, I can feel your dick going back and forth inside my pussy and my ass becomes even wetter. God you make me so fucking crazy, you fuck me so good! I'll never quite understand, but oh, you give me a hell of a fucking. You fuck my cunt and ass so good with your hard throbbing cock – penetrating my holes, you get me off more than I can count, but hay, who's keeping track – it's non-stop orgasms. You just don't stop pleasing me and I can never stop cumming, whether it's your mouth, fingers or your big hard dick, you do me so good and I just get wetter and wetter with every thrust.

Fucking my cunt the way you are, I place my fingertips over my clit and start rubbing myself – my fingers move so quickly, I feel as though a freight train is inside me. Gradually working its way forward, slowly picking up speed – rumbling with a measured, steady pace and then… my body begins to tremble and shake, rolling along the tracks and subsiding into the distance, only to find that you never lost your stead fast pace.

Suddenly we find our main rhythm – moving and grooving, building up and building up, breathing in and breathing out… until all at once a complete numbness comes over me – letting it all out with screams of abandonment, of pleasure and pain. The orgasm is so intense, so unbelievable, so shamelessly satisfying. I'm surrounded by such an aura; you've brought out such an explosion I've never experienced before – the rise, the crest, the fall are so unexpected I feel as if every muscle has become paralyzed – I can barely move, I am so comfortably numb.

Slightly moving inside me, helping me return to earth, to be conscious of reality, to feel once again – I am so aware of every inch of you. Rolling on to my back, I can only look at you with such awe; there is no need for words right now. I can feel your breath, your eyes – watching over me. You amaze me by how you bring out so much in me – things I never knew existed or were ever capable of achieving.

After a while of regrouping our minds and bodies, you were laying on your stomach, so I reach for the oil and write my name across your back – rubbing it in and trailing it down your legs, over your ass, my hands gliding over every inch of your beautiful body. Massaging your back, feeling every bit of you with my fingers and palms. You have such a strong back and rubbing you down turns me on and makes me wet. My thoughts drift away and I reminisce of how awesome you made me feel.

Wanting to please you and satisfy you because you gave me so much of yourself, I spread your cheeks apart and begin to lick your ass – up and down, round and round your hole. Thinking of how you lick me, I do the same to you. Darting my tongue in and out – further inside I push, spreading your cheeks farther apart the deeper I go, inching the tip of my tongue inside – licking you around, up and down. I hear you moan in pleasure and it makes me feel good.

I place a hand under your belly and put pressure there for you to rise up, following my lead, you are now on your knees and I get a better angle on your ass and just go with it – getting into it so good – enjoying it so much, pleasing you this way makes me so damn horny. Feeling the moisture I'm creating, kneading your cheeks with my hands, my tongue making you dizzy, slowly I slide myself under your leg to suck on your dick, as I do, I slip a finger into your wet ass and take your emotions for a ride.

Your ass is so wet and my mouth becomes so moist by sucking on your cock and playing with your ass. I know you'll be fucking me soon and the excitement begins to swell up in me. You'll slip your cock into my pussy until I get off, then you'll slide it in my ass, bringing me to orgasm.

As if you were reading my mind, you adjust yourself to enter me and Oh God – how it feels so fuckin good. "I'm your little cunt and you fuck my cunt so damn good. Fuck me – Oh baby – Fuck my cunt!" I can feel you pumping hard, thrusting your big cock fully inside my juice box. Back and forth, in and out, man you do me so fucking good. "I love the way you fuck me, don't stop – pleeaasse – don't stop." I want to hear you scream – let that freight train loose in your head, let go of it all and just feel us – together – our bodies joined, moving in unison.

I can feel your sweat dancing across my body like the rain that splashes down outside our window. Just flow with it – feel the sexual heat that radiates between us – lose yourself in our lovemaking, to the rhythmic churn of the wheels on the track. Release it, cum for me, fill me up inside.

At the same time as your rumble gathers to a piercing howl, I begin to let go of mine. I will hold on tight to you because hearing your screams only takes me to another height. I love the passion that comes out of you and I won't let go until you've surrendered to the calmness that begins to seep into your veins and takes over your body… mind and soul.

KISS OF LIFE

I CHERISH THE DAY when we get together – being around you places me into a mood of comfort and tranquility. You make my juices flow just by the sight of you, your clothes – the way your body looks in them, the subtle way your shirt lays upon your chest, how the blueness of your eyes reflects off the deep blue of your shirt. Your blue-jeans, just knowing what is underneath, the vision of your hardness – pushing and growing to get out. I want you from first sight, my body aches to be touched, the firmness of your grip kneading into my waist. The storm inside me begins to creep up, entering the flow in my veins.

As you're speaking, I watch the way your lips move, the exquisite way they're shaped and I think … how I'd love to press mine against them. The way they feel when they are sucking on my pussy and our juices mix and mingle, as the flow inside escalades – just to fill you up with such a sweet taste.

Longing to suck on you and trail my lips up and down your hardness, I've been looking at it to the point of staring. God how I want you so bad – is it a crime that I feel this way, wanting you like a good drug. My nipples have begun to peak, remembering how you tweak and twirl them between your fingers – can't you feel my body talking to you, you must see it! I'll just have to close my eyes and take myself on one of my pleasure cruises.

Imagining you there, the other night between my legs, playing with the ice in your mouth – you tell me to lie down, placing my head upon the pile of pillows that look so inviting. The coldness on my pussy lips sends my body to shivering, but not in a cold way – your hot mouth mixed with the chill temperature begins to make me nuts. Wanting you to caress every inch of me – erase my mind of all but the pleasures you bestow upon me. Licking me and sucking me, my hot juicy little pussy, wet like never before – I feel the moisture making its way down to my ass, soon after, your lips follow.

I feel your hands underneath my ass and thighs, ruling the way that I move, back and forth, almost rocking me, closing my eyes I tune into the way your tongue passes up and down, twirling around my ass, back to sucking on my lips, down again and then … catching my breath I feel a cube inside my asshole. Oh man, what a rush of sensations, you make me crazy and crazier with every movement, everything you do to me. I lose myself to the ecstasy that ripples through me, as if there is no gravity, but in a corner of my mind I am slightly aware of reality.

Opening my eyes to adjust myself to the surroundings, I see you up above, in the mirrors – reaching to stroke your beautiful body, hungry for your passion, thirsting for that distance. You look up and the light shines from your eyes like diamonds. I can get lost peering into them and then something in them leads me deeper into you. The state of mind you place me under is like the deepest ocean; my world dissolves into one long moment.

Wrapping your arms around my thighs, I arch my back because I feel the explosion that grows near, full of intensity, rushing up like lava that bursts from a volcano, spilling over into you. You move up to place my sweetness inside my belly button, as I watch you do this I gently touch it, dabbing my fingers in and about my cum. I swirl it around, then rub it into my stomach – so silky and pure. Tasting and sucking on my finger, watching you slither back down to my sweet spot, I gaze at you and stare intently at what you are doing. A swell of sensations courses down my spine, uncontainable no longer, I release the surge of all that you've built up inside me once again. The rush is magical, the journey – a mystical one, but now I know I'll have your dick inside me soon – the true connection of our bodies. The thought provokes many emotions inside of me.

Slowly I can feel you slipping into my smooth wetness, ahhh, this time I won't go astray, I'll watch you with my eyes wide open. I'll look up and see you fucking me – how your ass moves with every stroke into me. Placing my hands on your back, rubbing them down, feeling the muscle beneath my palms.

You show me how deep love can be, I breathe in your air – feeling as though only you can rescue me. I move with you, to the beat of your rhythm and together we begin the dance – bodies intertwined, your strong body on top of mine, feeling the drumming of your heart tapping on my chest.

You feel so good on top of me – fitting me perfectly, our bodies molding to a beautiful shape. Gently holding your butt, my hands hover over your ass, concentrating on the way your dick moves inside me, back and forth – up and down, you penetrate me deeper and for a minute longer each time.

The art of your lovemaking takes control of my senses, shifting and wavering – tossing me one way and another, moving in different directions like the blacks and blues of a daunting storm rolling in on the horizon. Wrapped in your arms – feeling safe – wrapping my legs through and over yours, locking myself in… I tumble towards ecstasy. Your kisses reign around my head, lightly across my ears, trailing over my lips. Whispering to you for more, my words soft and barely audible, capturing you for a deep passionate kiss, running my hands through your hair – defying the air we breathe.

As if the moon were high and full, we dance along the edge of the tide, whirling and leaping to our own beat of time. Holding onto you, fitting each other like a hand in glove, round and round you're touching me, making my soul sing. I'm so into you – you posses my body and take control over me completely. The motion increases, our bodies striving to reach that higher high – such a sweet surrender.

The quiet of the storm blows in and I never felt this hot before, you give me something that is taboo, anything you ask or want of me, don't let it slip away. We keep bringing out the best in each other and with a sudden clash of emotional bliss, we both erupt – shooting up as a firework would, igniting the horizon – spreading across the sky and then … sparkling downward, trickling down to the ground – dissipating over the earth and as the thunder would shout from the clouds, you release the crash and rumbles of your rising orgasm, just to become lost on the spiraling wind of your breath. Our bodies give in – relax and grow weak; the only sound left is the beating of our hearts.

MY TEDDY BEAR

MY BODY HAS BEEN aching for your touch, whether it is soft and subtle or hard and driven – the need is always there. So, on this misty chilly... rainy evening – the kind of night when I stepped outside to grab another log for the fire, I paused because the aroma of a damp fall November – the scent of smoke billowing in the air and mixing together, captured me for a brief... exotic – tantalizing spell. I breathed in deeply the wonders of a mystical night as this.

To set the tone, I decided to light some candles and placed them all around the bathroom. Running the hot water as it filled the area with steam and drizzling the bubbles underneath the spout. Opening the window just a bit so I can hear the rain, the smell from outside seeps in and I sat for a moment, savoring the thoughts of how when we're together and we play in the tub, oh, how the memories skip across my mind and I soon feel the tension subsiding away.

Submerging myself into the water, the warmth – the heat, gathers around my body and man, it feels divine... mmm. Suddenly I've retreated to another time, my thoughts carry my spirit away and I feel your hands caressing my body. Rubbing circles around my beautiful tits, wrapping your strong hands around my neck – then straight down my arms – up the inside of my thighs, your palm slips past my pussy.

Grabbing my waist with both hands, your fingers with

penetrating strength travel up my back and your thumbs curve their way under my plump titties to follow a path back down past my stomach. Stopping to swirl a finger around my belly button ... to their final destination as you slip a finger inside my pussy hole and my eyes pop open as I sit back with a chuckle, only to see my candles glowing all around me.

Shaking my head and grinning, I reach for the soap and begin to lather myself up, turning my body into a soapy – slippery wet – horny little girl. Smoothing the frothy white fluff up, down and beneath my arms, across my shoulders, back and forth – massaging, stroking – then up to the center of the back of my neck, with visions of how we fucked in my bed the other day.

You left a hot-n-juicy message on my phone, 'tell me you're going to get that wet pussy all warmed up and latch your arms to the bed post, bend over and beg for it, then I'll slam my hard throbbing cock into your juicy wet, dark hole – think about it won't you?' Hmm, you wanted it kinky, so I plotted and planned.

When you were undressing, I took my time so you'd be naked – in bed before me and able to watch. As I undressed, I could feel your eyes upon me, when I looked up with my bashful grin – you had been watching! I spied your hand gripping the bottom of your shaft and it was proudly at attention. "Hope you like what you see," I said, crawling towards you in my fishnet body – sinking lower until my mouth reached the bulls' eye.

Keeping my backside suspended in the air to give you a nice view, I reach out with both hands, holding your hardness, devouring your head only – in ... my ... mouth. My body begins to sway back and forth, as I want more of you I sink down to the bed – now flat on my stomach I hear your voice, how sweet that ass looks, so perfectly rounded and what a valley in between.

You sit straight up to smooth your hands over the holey fabric and as you do so, your cock plummets further down my throat – pressing you backwards with the palm of my hands for fear you'll choke me with such a manly cock – you move back. In the process, I roll onto one side still sucking on you – you reach out to the farthest point and rub your hands all the way up my body, into my hair, tousling it and pushing it away from my face – as you gaze down upon me, I glance up at you with a wink an a smile.

Bouncing up on my knees to go straight down on your dick, working myself slowly back up, you take a hold of my hips and direct me onto my back. I slide up the bed a little more while you slither towards me on your stomach with your hands between my thighs, pushing outward – you come in for a landing. Oh my heavens, taking a deep prolonged breath – slowly exhaling because 'DAMN'... you know just how to flip that switch – you are soo bad, but yet you are soo good!

Sucking my clit, whirling your tongue inside my pussy hole, your words reach my ears, "You juicy – hot – wet – dripping," licking me all around, spinning your tongue after each single word is spoken, "Bald – headed – coming all over the place – saaweet pusss... a!" You stick a finger inside for a scoop of sweet juice, ooh – you warm 'lil fucking pussy and then... you slide another finger just slightly up my ass to make me scream for more, at the same time your bearded face with soft bristles encircles my pussy.

The electricity zips through my veins – reaching out to you, I beg you to come to me – "Please fuck me... please... I want you inside of me, Oh, you are making me KAH – RAY – Zee!! I want your cock, not your fingers, even though they work so well, I want the real thing, Oh please give it to me, isn't that what you want to hear – me pleading for it?"

With a flash of lightning, you penetrate my warm – waiting honey cunt; the deep hard pounding of your cock brings forth the golden droplets. You lean in to kiss my lips and I see that your mouth is smeared with love juice, so I gladly receive both your tongue and a bit of honey. Pulling one strap down off my shoulder, releasing a round perky tit, you suck my nipple 'til it's taut and hard – fucking me much faster, I capture your waist and spread my legs wider. You let loose my other tit and swoop down to suck on that nipple, both of them are sticking straight up and bouncing back and forth, the visual for you is obviously good because you're slamming me even harder.

Taking a hold of my legs, you bring them up into the air – spread eagle – grasping the fishnet stocking, pulling it down – until it's off one leg, exposing my pussy full view to you. I reach for the hanging empty leg and stretch it across your back, holding onto it as our liaison becomes wickedly out of control. The rapture of our fucking is so wild and crazy, we seem to get lost in it and the world slips away except for the words exchanged between us and the heat that flows from your body to mine – man, you are such a good fuck.

Suddenly you pull out of me, in the midst of the craziness and bring forth your poker hard cock right to my lips – holding my head up to receive you... without hesitation I open up and say mmm, sucking on your dick, tickling your asshole and squeezing your ass cheeks, I hear you tell me that I'm such a good cock sucker. Laying yourself down, I curl up into the crook of your legs, I love to suck on you – you know it makes me happy that you think I'm such a good cock sucker. As you lay there taking it all in your husky voice states that I have very nice panels and in response to you I pump your balls and sheepishly giggle.

You decide to lay me cross wise over the bed, my head hangs over the edge just a bit, my nipples are sticking up like two little knobs – waiting and wanting to be tweaked – sucked and played with. As usual, you're always on it, so you take one perky nipple at a time – suckling each one, left to right – back and forth. At the same time your cock is sliding – grinding in and out of... 'Oh my gosh,' juicy pussy and in one swift move, you flip us around like the hands on a clock.

Now you are on the bottom, lying at the head of the bed and I get to be on TOP. Oh, what fun it is to ride – telling you that you're such a crazy fucking man! I start fucking the shit out of your cock, leaning forward – thrusting my tits in your face so you can do what you do best, licking – sucking – fucking and making me nuts. Wanting it more – wanting it faster, I grab onto the head board and ride like the wild cat that I've become. You start chanting, "Ride that cock – ride that cock – come on baby, ride it … ride it … ride it," until it all goes to my head; sucking me in further, your voice – your words, nothing but the fucking, grinding my clit in the space between your cock and belly, rubbing to get that burn – pushing deeper and faster.

I feel your hand inching across my ass cheek, your finger reaching and diving into my ass hole – "Oh my god, oh yeah, that's it, uh-huh, ooo … give it to me – come on, yeah – that's it, right there – right there – don't stop … please don't … Oh my." I throw my head back and let out a hell cat of a scream … "Whoa, my word, oh my – man … I had to, I couldn't bear it any longer, you kept building me up and pushing me onwards, it was like crazy mad – you drew me into it – sucked me in until I was so over the edge. WOW … that was fantastic!"

With shaking hands and revved up nerves, I strip off the rest of my fishnet outfit, coming down and trying to get my bearings from that mind-blowing orgasm, I definitely know it has served its purpose. You tell me to lie down on my back, breathless and moving methodically until you, slowly but surely, slide into my pussy with a satisfied ahhh – you sweet … wild little cat, I can feel your body purring. Wrapping my arms around your back while you begin your flight to the final destination, I can feel my heart beating inside your chest. You speak to me in hushed tones of how I fucked your cock so good; you're a sweet piece of ass and now it's your turn to make me crazy and cum.

Lowering your head down into my shoulder, I begin to whisper in your ear – you beautiful fucking man, you're so good to my pussy, I love that I can let go with you and just fuck the shit out of your cock; meanwhile I'm licking the edge of your earlobe … mmm and you let me – let me let go, you give me the reins to go with it, to have the freedom, to be a horny … cunt, oh man – your cock feels great inside me.

That's it baby – talk to me, tell me how you get it so good, tell me whose cunt you are, talk to me and make me cum. Tell me how your pussy loves a hard throbbing cock, you hot juicy box, your pussy is so warm, inviting – hot and dripping wet, I could scoop it out with a spoon and suck it up. Even as you're speaking to me you slide your hand under my ass until your finger reaches my asshole and ohh, ooo – you know what that does to me. So you start to tickle and strum it, making me wriggle around. "Oh, you are such a naughty man!"

I feel my pussy begin to tighten up on your cock as your finger twirls around the outside of my hole; I bring my leg up to give you better access and taking my lead, you slide your finger in deeper. I squeeze your cock with my pussy as you delve further inside, "Oh man – Oh you dirty fuck – you fuck me so good, you know just how much of a teasin' I need to get me all worked up and then you know exactly how to please me while you fuck my hot … juicy … puss-A, Oh so fuckin' good … mmm – give it to your baby, Oh yeah."

I catch a glimpse of your face – I can tell that you're getting closer to the edge, so I keep talking to you – spinning you into my web of words, of seduction while you fuck my cunt, slamming and jamming. "Oh yeah, you hot fucking man, come on – give it to me, your sweet baby wants it bad," my arms extend outward and I slip my hands into the opening of the bedpost to hold on. My tits are bouncing with perked up nipples and your face is showing all signs of an explosion. "Give me your cock, deep – down and hard, that's it, fuck me – fuck me – fuck your cunt, I know you're there, come on you big fucking cock, award your treasure chest a little gold, I want it soooo bad, I want it all, your pussy needs it oh so … oh" and you rupture with an orgasm that could shake the earth.

My body experiences the jolts zipping through you – your shriek resounds off the walls and reverberates all the way through my veins – Holy Shit – your like a freight train out of control with the longest, winded scream I have ever heard, from out of your mouth. Man, that is some serious stuff there. Collapsing on top of me in total exhaustion, your breathing is harsher than mine when I had exploded and I thought I had a hell of an orgasm.

I stroke your body, removing the sweat beads from you, to calm you and shush the effects that riveting orgasm gave you. In breathless words, you whisper, "I have no idea where that came from" and with a mischievious laugh, I reply, "It's okay – I think I kind of know and it doesn't matter because … you are absolutely amazing."

SATURDAY

THE HORNY CREEP BEGAN its crawl as I was biding my time yesterday with thoughts of 'until we meet again.' The full force of the storm would be upon us tomorrow, but for today... the wind was blowing wildly like the fantasies through my mind.

Noticing the strong winds moving the treetops as I made my way to you, a strange sensation trickled through my veins. Always the same place and the same time, meeting you like this makes my heart skip a beat and my stomach does somersaults because I know once we're together, our true rendezvous will begin.

Rain wickedly danced across my face as I darted for your truck, stepping in and laughing with a bit of amusement, it felt as though your sweat had moistened my skin as it so often does when we get hot -n -heavy. The atmosphere felt eccentric and my body was electrified. 'Oh my,' I thought to myself, it's going to be one of those days.

Conversing with each other, venturing to our spot, you told me of trees being down across the road. There was a detour that took you through the muddy back roads and you shook your head all the while asking, 'All this just for pussy... is it really worth it.' I told myself as we were locking ourselves in for the morning that I'd make it worth your while.

Turning both showers on to a comfortable setting, I proceed to make a drink for us. Moving towards the window as if drawn to it, I take a peek at Mother Nature and pause at the awe of her fury. I'm so turned on by the power of the storm that I absently turn to look at you, becoming absorbed in your eyes and going deep into them.

Recalling thoughts of how I want to play in the shower with you. To feel your body pressed against mine at the same time as your finger slips into my ass-hole, so ready and wanting. As if you were reading my mind, you tell me to come on … enough of the gazing, we've got better things to do with our time.

Squatting against the wall, my legs open and willing – I beg you to come to me. "Please give me what I've been missing and waiting for … please relieve those pent up hornies inside me." And as usual, you are so happy to oblige. Oh the rush of it actually happening, the thrill rippling about my senses. I become still, yet the motion carries me farther … deeper. Leaning my head back for support my eyes drifting half shut, your finger dips in and out so effortlessly.

RELAX … s l o w d o w n; I don't want to rush this. You see, when I get to this point – time stands still – nothing around, all but vanished … and you … there you are. Chasing me onward, leading me all around just because you know I will follow … I am gone – eyes closed, aware only of my private escape. Your lips suckle each of my erect nipples, arching my back for more attention. Your fingers diving in and out of my hole with such rhythm and matched grace to you're nuzzling on my tits. You know exactly where you're taking me and I'm all for the ride. The blast of sensations erupts, swirling over … under … throughout and across my body. "Oh yeah – oh man – that's it – Oh gosh, it's so fucking good." Holding on to you with one arm, I wrap myself into you – molding our bodies to one connected core. Your words echoing in my ear, "You sweet little ass hole, you wanted it finger fucked so bad, didn't you?" "Uh -uh – yes, please, give it to me!" "Oh I am, you wet fucking ass – I'm giving it to you real good and I got more just because you are such a horny little piece of ass." And overboard I tumble into a whole new plateau.

Releasing your body, I crumble towards the wall, but

your finger stays connected. In an instant I am aware of the difference – you've slipped two fingers inside me! Easing into it slowly, relishing the idea that my senses are going to be heightened furthermore, I reach for the baby oil and squish it over your chest as your thumb tickles my clit. "Oh you are such a very bad man!"

Giggling naughtily, taking a hold of the showerhead and placing the stream directly on my clit, I sink deeper...headed for the depths of sweet pleasure. "Oh you finger fucking devilish man, it feels so good and you are so amazing." Rapidly rising to the explosion that was bound up, small and tight, a whirlwind of exotic emotions displays across my face. Everything feels as if it is happening in slow motion. Your lips suckling my nipples – the water caressing my clit – your fingers sliding... sliding... and gliding, breathing Oh and breathing Ah. Tumbling towards...reaching for... "Oh yeah, Oh that's it"...rising higher becoming elevated, until "O – O – Ohhhhh" – releases from my lungs and reverberates off the four walls, ripping through our ear drums. Your finger slows its pace while my hand releases the showerhead...silence descends upon us except for the sounds of our hard breathing, once again the moment held me imprisoned.

Sinking back against the wall, my body feels like it has been lifted away – carried off – floating serenely with the clouds, the energy surfing through my body is unbelievable. A sigh escapes my lips as I look at you and I can't help but to be in a state of mind. It is you – all because of you.

When we connect, there are no words that can describe the ultimate highs you deliver to me. The feeling of euphoria, the rush of sensations... I just close my eyes, keep my mind open and away I go. I know you are there with me because you are the one taking me there. Oh man, there is nothing like the feeling of being totally one with each other, mentally united, physically bonded and soulfully joined.

"Thank you so very much for that – my asshole sends its thanks too!" Looking at me through sedated eyes, laughing and telling me that I am one funny little girl, you pull me into you with a grasp of possession and captivate my lips.

Making our way out of the shower and onto the bed, I can only anticipate where this fantastical ride will lead. Since I am already feeling crazy – I decide to put on a sexy little outfit for you. Glancing over at you sprawled out on the bed, I notice your body is glistening from the baby oil. I spy your massive hard on – your strong hand stroking it up and rubbing it down, holding your shaft as you grab a handful of your balls. Oh yeah – we're going to tear this place apart; I can feel it in the air!

Slipping my body into the V of your legs, I lick your head while you still have a hold of your cock in your hand. Playfully teasing, you tap the head of your dick on my lips as I stick my tongue out and try to suck you inside. Taking a hold of what I want, your hand remains on top. Keeping your head in view I run my tongue 'round-n-round,' in circles across your fingers at the same time as I suck on your hardness.

Removing your hand completely, I finally have all the access I want. I fully grasp your cock and have at it. This is my favorite past time – I love to suck on your cock because I know you aren't going to cum and I can have as much fun as a kid in a candy store. Drooling over my biggest lollipop, mm-mm-good!

Kneeling between your legs, I put all play aside and suck you with so much fervor; I begin to feel my pussy pulsating. Your hand darts out to fondle my tit but I back away. I don't want to be touched just yet. I want this to be all your pleasure – lean back and enjoy. I love to be able to just suck on you without being touched because the less you touch me, the more want – the more crazier and hornier I get. Focusing all my attention to your cock, builds up that itch to go wild on you!

Moisture seeps from my mouth, trailing down your shaft onto my hand, so I take it and rub it all over your cock. Man, I get so fucking wrapped up and lost – the only thing that matters is sucking on that nice…big…hard…throbbing…COCK!! I enjoy this immensely and I can feel my pussy starting that twitching to get fucked.

Letting go of your stiff, wet cock, inching off my lace thong, I make my way towards you. You seem to think that I'm going to fuck you because you grab a hold of your shaft for safe landing. As I pass it by, I say to you, "Oh No, buddy, this is only the beginning, I'm not ready for that. My pussy is dripping with sweet juicy droplets... I'm headed for your face." Straddling your head, you sink into the pillows for a better position. I hear you rumble softly with an animal sound to it as I put my cunt directly on your lips. "Oh Baby... Oh yeah... now this is what I want!!"

"That's it... you sweet pussy sucker – suck on my pussy, drink from my juice box." Just like I lost myself to your cock, you seem to be doing the same with my cunt. Looking down into the depths of your eyes – your face... so beautiful and perfect, whilst piercing blue eyes looked back. Flashes of interesting magnetism zip all the way through my body. God... I am so easy – to be able to cum just by looking into you. Lifting my face to the ceiling exclaiming, "Oh I just can't help it," while running a hand throughout my hair, a hand over your forehead and fondling my tits as you tilt me back. "Yes... Oh yeah... you are so good to my puss, mmm... man, you make me fucking crazy... Oh God, you fucking pussy sucker!!"

Staying connected to my cunt, you lean me backwards until I'm on my back and Oh Shit, I can't believe you just did that without stopping the divine pleasure you are exquisitely delivering to me. Positioned on my back, I place a foot in the crook of your waist and gingerly you roll me onto my side still tantalizing my screaming pussy. I am so amazed at what you did, I cannot believe throughout all that we stayed as one and your lips never left my cunt. Heaven... I must be in Heaven!

Stroking a finger into my asshole – still sucking my pussy, I feel as if I'm melting in a cauldron of hot weakness. The magic you swirl around my soul creates an intoxication of being as elevated as a harvest moon on All Hallows Eve. The dance your tongue and finger are dancing sears my body as if I were leaping on the tip of the flames. "Oh for mercy's sake, you're making me fucking crazy, you suck on me so freaking good – oh shit – you horny fucking man … I can't believe you do what you do to me. Oh, I am such a lucky little girl."

Bringing me back to some sort of realization, you rest yourself on top of me. S L I D I N G that massive, beautiful, rock hard cock into your juicy, oh so wet; slippery, silky smooth pussy. Rumbles of satisfaction seep from inside you. Gliding your soft stubbly moist beard around my cheeks, licking my lips from corner to corner, rubbing your chin over mine and making my entire face wet with my own sweet juice. Your fingers fumbling with the satin bow in between my tits to expose them fully and you push my teddy to the wayside. Smacking my lips together and tasting myself, I pull you closer into me and run my tongue over your lips as we tangle in each other's arms.

Ravishing my lips, our kiss turns primal. Sliding off me just a bit, your lips capture my tit and you suck on my hard nipple. Reaching my hand down to grab a hold of your ass, you lift yourself up onto your arms. Running my hand across your broad chest, I intertwine my fingers throughout the chains on your neck, tugging on them with slight pressure.

Grabbing up one of my legs, nipping on my skin, you rest it over your shoulder. Still fucking and staying together, I move onto my side, bringing my leg to your other shoulder. As I do this you slide the tip of your finger into the entrance of my asshole and tease me until the inevitable happens.

"Get on your knees," I hear you say. Dreamily shifting around, you continue to fuck my cunt, grabbing a hold of my tits and tweaking my nipples, you send me into over drive. I feel your hand take hold of your cock and slowly ease it into my asshole. "Take it like a good girl now – you know you're going to enjoy this and it will only be for a little because it won't be long before your ass cums all over my cock." Sure enough with a couple of long … deep strokes, I release that wonderful spine tingling eruption.

Leaning backwards, you take a hold of my waist and guide me with you. Once I'm on top of you, reaching between my legs,

I seize your cock and slip it inside my pussy. Bending forward, staying on my knees and resting on my arms, I look through to see your shaft disappearing and reappearing. Oh gosh, I can't watch for very long because ... Oh man – I'm going to spill over again. At the same time as I'm cumming, you waste no time in dipping a finger into my asshole, only to heighten this craziness going on inside my loins and "Oh shit ... you know what that's going to do to me, Oh fuck, Oh god, Oh yeah ... don't stop, please ... Oh my goodness, that was purrfect!"

Pivoting around your body, pausing every once in a while to stroke my pussy on your cock until I totally face you. Digging my feet under your legs for a tighter fit, I cradle your head and bring it to my tits. In the position to ride – ride on little girl – my pussy delves into your cock and onward I go. In my glory, fucking you with all that I got, your lips suckling each of my nipples, giving them all the attention they need. I thrust further and farther, craving and reaching for that elevation my cunt seeks every time we fuck! Lost on the whirlwind of sweet intoxication, I raise myself up, toss back my head and howl to the heavens ... collapsing over your body in a rumpled mess and breathing as if the wolves were at my feet.

Embracing me with your strong arms and sitting up, your cock sinks deeper into me. I put my feet together around your backside as you rock me slowly, holding me against you – enclosed in our small world ... kissing me so affectionately gazing in each other's eyes. Pausing for a mind-shattering kiss, your emotional display burns deep into my soul.

Steadying me onto my back, your beautiful body encloses mine as your cock lies atop my pussy, leisurely stroking it. Holding you tightly in my arms, whispering in your ear how incredible I think you are ... such a marvelous pussy sucking you have given me and what a glorious fucking you delighted my senses with. You are magnificent ... wonderfully unbelievable and I am the luckiest little cunt ever!!

Just as the day turns to night, you begin thrusting your cock with renewed intensity and making my throat tighten with anticipation. "Yeah that's it, you sweet pussy – take some cock." "Oh please… give it to me, you beautiful fucked up man, come on, please fuck my cunt – fuck it – fuck it – fuck it!"

Your voice harsh and possessed, "You're mine… you little cunt, you belong to me," while your hand cups my face and your wild eyes consume mine. "Tell me who fucks you – tell me who gives you such a good cock. I own your pussy, you hot fuckin' cunt – YOU ARE MINE. Speak to me… come on – huh – tell me… tell me who fucks you, my sweet little piece of ass." "You do… you do – Oh gosh – you fucking fuck my cunt. I belong to you, my cunt is yours… you own my pussy, you rule my cunt… TAKE IT… fuck it, come on – Oh yeah, fuck it baby, fuck me you fuck."

Losing stability, our words zip up one way and then another, meeting in the center and doubling back, spiraling down our bodies, inflating into levels of rapture, chasing our thoughts with a focus so powerful it's only a matter of time before we combust.

"Oh please don't stop, you fucking man, yeah that's it, please give it to me, I want it so bad, give it to me please… I want your cum, I want your explosion – I want to feel your cum filling me up." Raggedly breathing, I erupt with a sound of a wild primitive wail and at the same time you explode with a R…O…A…R that fills the room.

Your palm damp in my hair, feeling sweat intermingling, all that we hear is the sound of our hearts as our chests rise and fall in worn out rhythm. Seeking your hand and locking fingers as our breathing slowed, your body softened and relaxed across mine but held me down with gentle, solid weight. Touching your cheek, tracing the line of your jaw, following the firm curve of it down to your chin and up across your lips. You turn to kiss me; your breath is warm and heavy on my skin.

In silence, I recall the sound of your laughter, how priceless in its rarity, and your kisses, just as precious in their abundance. You are a beautiful man… a sensual, vital man – you speak volumes with out ever saying a word. You enfold me in your arms and draw me in as close as you possibly can, wrapped up in our sanctuary... we are in pure and simple peace.

BURNING DESIRE

CHAOTIC AND CRAZY… that's how life has been for you lately and the anxiety… my sexual anxiety, has been building everyday. I feel as though my body is being deprived. Tilting my head back, breathing in deeply, I look to the sky and let it all out in a swift rush. Sitting here with the sun and the sea, on this quite beach, my fingers begin strumming, my toes slightly tapping and my thoughts… well… that is a whole different world right now.

I want you so bad I can taste it! I need you to be right and rough so much, I can feel it. Handful of my hair, pulling my head back – spanking my ass and telling me how you're going to fuck me up and down and every which way – saying you're going to give me the show. Well, damn it, I'm dying for it all! Man… I can feel you right now – right here, as the breeze skims over my body, so do your strong hands.

Overpowering my self-control, you lead me down paths I know oh so well, but this… this path is becoming overgrown and strewn with thorns as the way your life has. Yeah, you hot fucking man, thrust your cock deep into my pussy so it feels like it's coming out my throat. Reaching a hand out I tenderly push through this murkiness that clouds me, amazingly I sense no pain. My body is longing for this kind of fucking. Trample over these jumbled vine patches, take the clutter away from my body and mind… make it disappear into the abyss. Rock me up and down, stroke it in and out, and slap my ass. Yeah, that's it, come on you big fuckin cock. Give me what I want ... my pussy craves it so bad.

Lifting my head to pause, I focus on the scenery. Noticing how the waves are crashing madly down onto the shoreline is exactly the way I want to get fucked. The intensity they create is a power I know so very well and a force I long to feel. Damn, just sitting here ... I let myself go so deep and far away. I am so connected to you sexually that as I think ... I feel. I am quite familiar with your touch. I have experienced sexual gratification, over and over again because of you. By reminiscing of those wild encounters, I do believe I experience what you have burned into my soul. Passing through my body, bringing you to life, seeing you, fucking me ... almost as it was. I hunger after you so fucking bad that my mouth moistens and my cunt juices begin to flow.

Flip me over and let the loving begin. Your back so broad and strong ... mmm, licking my lips as I take a taste of your shoulder. Burrowing your head in my hair – breathing deep my scent. Kiss me, you hot man, take control of my mind as your tongue probes and pushes with those oh so sweet lips. You mesmerize me ... crystal blue eyes, shooting prisms of fantastic light, that's it, let me see those eyes come to life. Drawing me into you and out ... into the listless, floating orb that creeps its way around our bodies – encompassing us both.

Your hand slides under my cheek and your finger tickles the entrance to my asshole. "Oh, you know how crazy that makes me." Give it to me anyway – you are such a bad boy and I quiver with the thoughts of what will happen next. You remove me from reality and you mend the aches that haunt me. "I love when that naughty man comes across your being." I know the change in you – I always can feel the shift in your body. Do me as you will, I just want to get fucked anyhow you see fit.

The hunger within takes a hold, your hands grasping me tighter, utterly constricting me. I'm wound up small and tight and all I'm aware of is this constant need to get fucked and to be fucked! "God, I am so fucking horny – I lust for every part of you!!" Untie this cord – as the center of my unit caves in. Pound my pussy... give it to me hard and deep, unravel the animal that has awakened. I want to feel the burn, buried under your possession. Please, I am screaming inside so loudly – your body should feel the piercing. "Make crazy mad love to me; fuck the shit out of my cunt. Give it to me... all of it; I am so blinded by my desire for you." I sink and swirl with every touch you give me.

Even though you're fucking my pussy so good, I have this overwhelming urge to get on top of you. I want to be in control, I want to be in charge of the show for a little while. I'm going to ride your cock into the sunset and pound it along where the ocean meets the sand. I want to lose all sense of rhyme... reason... and sanity.

Straddling your hard cock, wasting no time in pushing my tits into your face, you take a nipple in between your teeth and pinch gently, but enough for me to experience the high. "Mmm, yeah – now that's what I'm talking about. Suck on my tits you fuck. Suck harder and then swirl my nipple around your tongue." Arching my back, savoring this wonderful sensation, involuntarily I take away my titties from your mouth, but instantly your hand grabs a hold of my ass and you squeeze, nice and tight.

"Oh, you sweet fucking man, grab that nice Italian ass – hold onto it and push my cunt further into your cock. Slide a finger in my asshole... please... I want that stirring emotion." I want to experience that mad rush that comes over me when all these things are happening at once. I am such a horny little cunt and I need to have it, I got to have what you do to me. Pushing your finger into my asshole, I lean into your face again. Cradling your head in my hand – bringing your mouth directly to my titties, instinctively you know what I'm after. "Oh Yeah, a – huh, m - hmm... that is exactly what I fuckin crave, totally what I've been dying to feel."

Our movements take on their own course, sucking, fucking – fingering my ass and I'm licking my lips completely absorbed in all that is going on. "Riding your cock so good and it feels so fucking fine! Oh, you beautiful fucked up man ... come on you, you sweet fuck, give your little slut just what it wishes. Fuck me ... fuck me ... ohh, don't you stop, please." I am fuck ... ing your cock, oh so freaking good, yeah – riding it like an untamed mustang fresh from the crossing. "Getting it so good and your giving it so great."

I'm headed for the deep end, one more wave to splash over and under me and Oh god ... here I go. I have lost control; it's all just happening so swiftly and crazily, my body – my mind, all turned out and jumbled – everything taking place, the gathering – the ascent – the elevation. "Come on baby, talk to me ... tell me how bad I am. Speak to me of how much of a horny cunt I am. Tell me who owns my pussy ... tell me who fucks me the best." Ahh, yeah, push me onward with that voice of yours. Call me to the other side and make me drown in our dizzy noise.

Our voices mixed and mingling, stroking my cunt on your cock, words twisting and thrown about. Leveling off and realizing that I am going to descend, all the havoc of my kept in frenzy from not being fucked spills from my lungs. I begin in an edgy tone with teeth clenched; speaking through my lips, because the depth of this orgasm is being pulled from the darkness and it is has been locked away for far too long. "Oh my, oh man ... I am going to cum ... all over ... your big cock" and then the screech ... "O, Oh, Uhhhhhhh ... Ahhhhhh, God! Oh my fucking gosh!" Abruptly it all ceases and I try to grasp for my bearings. With haphazard breathing, collapsing on top of you and an oh shit, man, that was fucking awesome!

Swiping my face across your dampened chest, I look up at you with the biggest heartfelt grin. Inching myself towards your face, to kiss your lips gently, thank you and so very softly, thank you for that, for that wonderful release. Once again you have set me free.

Turning me onto my back, you slip your cock into my juice box. Still catching my breath, I warn you that I feel like play dough. With a shitty grin you reply, "Than all the better to do with you as I please." Reminding me of how horny I am and that you are not finished yet, you press and mold your hands over my plump tits and push down. Everything escapes me and as I took that first swift breath, it is now a gust of wind from my lips.

"I know you aren't finished and as for myself, you know that I'm such a bad girl… I'll take all that I can get and even if I couldn't take it, I'd still want it!"

"Well then, show me how bad that little girl can be. It's your turn to push me out of this funk I've been in."

Raising my hips, I pull you into me. Hold on; hold onto me, for this is going to erase all the hell you've been through. Ravishing your lips… kissing you with as much fervor and passion as I can generate into you. My hands begin at your shoulders – to press and clutch, to your sides – soaking in your strength, rubbing down to your waist, encircling your body to mold into mine. Reaching further for your ass, grabbing a hold and pumping you cheeks, pushing you into me. "You hot fucking man." God, I love when your cock is inside me and we're so wrapped up in each other's embrace that there is hardly any room for breathing.

"Please fuck my horny cunt; I've been waiting and wanting this so bad." I know how to push you and pull you under into my current. I will drift with you and sink into your dimness because I know you'll triumph in the end. Entangled… our bodies lay, starting our journey upwards.

I've been thirsting for you so much, wanting you in the worst way, come on, come into me. "Fuck me, you sweet cock." Your cock is plunging deep into my cunt so good. Now… now you are mine and I'm going to wrap you up in my arms; in my body and love you like you have never known. I'll show you how sweet love can be, let me be the calm you seek, just give yourself to me and be free. Entranced from the words flowing off of my lips, your body speaks volumes to mine.

Laying yourself back, you place a leg straight across my shoulders and I do the same to you. Our bodies joined together, cock in cunt. Continuously fucking me as we move along, in no way stopping or taking your hard cock out of me. You lean up on your elbow – gripping the top of my thigh never letting me go, pushing in and out.

Whispering how hot and horny you have been for my sweet cunt. Telling me your going to fuck me every which you can. Rolling onto my side, staying attached to each other, our strokes carry on to this new position. Moaning in sweet delight, "Oh man, you are so fucking good to my pussy." You make me feel like…there just aren't enough or any words to convey this kind of high that you deliver into my body. Just pure fucking bliss!

Completely on my stomach now, you push your cock deep in to my cunt. Fucking me like this for a while until I beg for more, your feet tap at my legs and I close them together. "How's this for your juicy cunt, huh?" Squeezing my legs to tighten them a bit, I get to feel your strong hard cock in between my ass cheeks on through to my pussy. In and out…in and out you plunge deeper and harder with each stroke.

Automatically I raise my hips and suddenly your hand finds my clit. Your other hand reaches in for my tit and encloses over both of them, as your fingers rest near my mouth. You have your face in the crook of my neck and mine is facing yours, I feel your breath raspy by my cheek. My hair is tousled – intertwined through my fingers, encircled in yours. Your hand tickles my clit, at first slightly, but then rapidly you pursue it -the fucking you bestow on my being renders me elsewhere. I know exactly what I'm feeling but it's all happening at once and quickly, you twirl me like cotton upon the wheel. Round and round my emotions spin. "Oh yeah, you fuck me so good," my voice almost crying, "Please don't stop."

"You sweet fucking cunt, I have no intentions of stopping. You are mine and I will fuck you to the end. I want what I want too and I'm going to get it because you give it so innocently and openly. Oh you sweet precious piece of ass, I love fucking your cunt, you're my little pussy…so warm and welcoming."

Flipping me over – straddling on top of me and clasping your hands into mine, stretching them outwards. Look at those beautiful round tits, swooping in to suck on each one, erecting my nipples to a perfect peak. "Man, you make me fuckin nuts, fucking crazy; I just want to fuck the shit out of you! You are my sweet cunt – mine and only mine."

Our eyes locked, an unbreakable deep stare, no words between us, the world disappears and it's just you and me in our faraway place. Your cock glides effortlessly in and out of my pussy. My juices flowing like a river, twisting around your cock. My arms have a firm grip on your body, inching up, down... sideways, all over – any way.

Your hand slides under my ass, to enter inside. Taking all I can, I make it easy for you to access my asshole. Picking up my hips as your pounding cock dives deeper into me, I'm so lost to this crazy, round about, head spinning unleashing. "Fuck, this feels so fucking good – god – please don't stop." Taking a moment to suckle on my nipple and then back to my lips for a lingering kiss.

Words begin to flow from my mouth, I can't help it but I can't stop it. I know you want this to last as long as you can make it, I know you want to fuck more – but this is uncontrollable. I'm so enveloped in this fantastical ride that the words, they just keep flowing out. I love everything that's happening, the more I talk – the more I build up another explosion inside of me and, it's so right... it's everything I had hoped for and more.

I know I should stop, but – "Oh god, you fuck... you fuck, you sweet fucking cock." "I want your cock, oh – I want your cock... cum inside me, you big fuckin cock... cum inside me, oh, so good – um yeah, please give it to me. Sweet fucking man, give me your cum, I want your cum so bad – give it... give it... oh yeah... give it to me pleeaassee... "

Knowing I'm going to push you over as well as myself, our expressions spill out and our yearning for the light at the end reaches its crest. I begin crying out in sweet surrender, I hear the distant rumblings of yours overpowering mine and tighter we clasp to one another. The winding passageway of our voyage, the plateau of our sexual union has come to its climax.

Bursting and rupturing we both let out wails of pent up overdue emotions, as if they were demons being released from their dwellings. Clinging tightly together, our bodies radiant and shimmering like embers that had burned hot – as though we danced in and about through the fire, felt cool to the touch. So much passion given and taken, and such an alluring spell to be placed under.

Dreamily drifting away, I whisper softly in your ear. Rolling on to your side, you scoop me into you and wrap your arms so tightly, snug and secure around my body that I know I am home, for there is no other comfort than being here with you... like this.

I'M SO LUCKY

THE WAY YOU FUCK me is so good – the rhythms we create together are the best I've ever experienced. You move my body like never before, I follow you stroke for stroke, slide to grind. Raising my hips higher to match your level until we connect and in that moment we both realize – YES – this is where we want to be.

Your hands wrapped around my waist, guiding me – holding on as you give me such a good fucking. The chills that run up and down my spine, the need to have more, the blinding lights in my eyes – Oh Yeah, right there, fuck my pussy, make it slippery and slopping wet like only you know how to. Take me away from here; wrap me up in the colors of the setting sun. Pleasure mounts up, riding it all the way, leading me into a universe where I can only feel my heart beating in time with yours – against yours, just as your throbbing cock pulsates inside my soft warmth, making it wetter and hornier. So hard and big – gliding in, sailing out – picking up the pace, finding the earth shattering spot and bringing me to a frenzy of excitement.

Sliding me to the edge of the bed, you reach for something – placing it in your mouth, lowering ever so slowly towards my pussy. The coolness seeps out as you suck on me, stinging and numbing my clit, licking me up and down – the juices are flowing, making me so unbelievably wet, the cum and water mixed in your mouth, drips like a juicy popsicle – melting and trailing down your chin. You push the ice inside me as your tongue follows, swirling it around – fucking me with your tongue until I'm out of control. Darting in and out, pushing the ice farther until the heat inside me consumes it and you drink in my juices, spilling some down into the valley of my ass.

Pushing my legs up, your hands grip underneath my thighs, rocking me … then suddenly there's more ice, teasing my asshole this time. Feeling your tongue play around my hole with the ice – your mouth and tongue spin my world away. The way you make me feel all over, so many rushes and such high euphoria. Your tongue pushes the ice further, your lips circling around my ass like the rhythm of a ferris-wheel and the wetness begins to pour out as my ass is suspended in the air – I feel it trickling down the valley, towards my back.

Everything you do to me pleases me so much; I close my eyes and hold onto anything in my reach. Your blue eyes crinkle in humor and melt into me as you watch me go through my passage of pleasure, knowing full well that you are in control of the flight you are taking me on, of what is being written across my face. Slowly I begin to sink deeper and fade away farther into the swells. Inching me up more onto the bed, I open my eyes, look past my belly and watch as you enter me. BLISS and fulfillment gather in circles between my legs. Your hard cock, always at attention – so big and so ready, fucking my pussy so good – how you do the things you do is beyond me.

As soon as you enter me, no matter which hole you choose – I always lose myself to you, to my surroundings and slowly it all creeps back through my veins, feeling your body above mine – watching you fuck me, looking into your eyes. Bringing your body closer to mine, arms wrapped around me tight – your masculine scent permeates my being, I feel your breath on my skin and hear the spoken words of our sexual union coming off your lips … "You little cunt, you love to be fucked – who's cunt are you?" "Yeah, I am a cunt and I love to be fucked by you, I'm your cunt, only yours." Grasping a hold of my earlobe with your teeth, gently nibbling and saying those words to me, hearing your breathing, feeling the heat from your lips … making me absolutely insane, I explode and turn to jelly.

Sensing my yielding, you slip a finger into my asshole, preparing it, making it juicy and wet. Turning me on my stomach, your finger glides right in – the anticipation builds and builds – reaching higher to the itching spot. You take your dick in your hand and begin to move your head up and down, back and forth over my hole – around in circles. Suddenly your big hard cock slides into my wetness. Your dick feels so good in my ass – you make my body come alive.

I position myself better by bringing my hips up so I can feel your rhythm, the motion of how you glide in and out, making me wetter. God … how you feel so damn good! I lift my butt up just a little more until I'm on my knees. I ask why – "Why do you fuck my ass so good?" "You know I like fucking you, fucking your ass – you take it so good and I taught you everything you know – you never knew how good it was until I showed you."

With all those words and the constant, steady rhythm you've kept up, I give myself to you completely. Your fingers glide down my spine, a bare tickle that makes my breath come shallow and quick – "Fuck my ass, you fuck it so good – chase away the goose bumps, but don't stop fucking me until you can't take it anymore … until you feel the need to release it all inside of me and I can feel that time is … Oh, so near."

Your grip around my waist becomes a little stronger; your breathing more raspy, you smack each side of my ass cheeks just once, but the sting is even and perfect. The size of your cock throbbing inside me … the sweat that rolls off you onto my back, oh yeah, I know it's coming. I relax totally so you can fuck my ass with a steady motion for as long as you can and as you near your final thrust, I feel your body tremor – hear your screams as you gradually lay yourself on top of me and surrender to the ecstasy of erupting in my ass.

ENJOY THE HIGH

WE DROVE UP TO the top of the hill overlooking the fields – there was a stream below with the sound of spring peepers all around us in a serenade. The sun was just setting and the colors in the sky were colliding into the clouds. It was a beautiful evening and the urgency to see each other was apparent for the both us, an opportunity we didn't want to miss!

I stood, leaning against your truck, with my back to you listening to the music. I feel you coming up behind me, slipping your hands up my shirt and me, of course, not wearing a bra, gave you full access to my breasts. You begin to fondle them – then tweaking and twirling my nipples. I whisper how horny you are making me and I begin to rub my ass back and forth against you, feeling the hardness protruding from your shorts.

Laying the towel on the ground that you just happened to have, you ask me to lie upon it. But I couldn't wait any longer to have you... in my mouth. As you stand there dropping your shorts to the ground, I bend over and begin to suck on your dick, already so hard and oh so suckable. Man, I've missed sucking on you – holding your balls in my hand, I just suck on you with such pleasure that my mouth begins to drool. You reach down into my shorts and start to finger me. I am so wet and so horny for you that after a while of playing, I feel my legs getting weak and mentally – I need to have you, now!

I make my way to lie down, taking off my shorts as I watch

you lower yourself onto me. Your hardness penetrates my softness – you begin to love my body so gently and so slowly. I feel every inch of you and I can hear the motion of our lovemaking because I'm so wet. I breathe deep the scent that surrounds you – the manly smell of your body and feel your breath upon my face. This is so awesome, being out in the open like this – you are so awesome. Up above, the sky is so pretty, the sounds of nature all around us – peacefully making love outside, just you and I, under the heavens.

I can't bear the silence no more and begin speaking to you – how you feel so great, how you fuck me so good. How I've missed your dick inside of me. The sensations you always bring to life in me – I needed this so bad. Knowing that my words may bring you to an orgasm, I just can't stop whispering the sexual desire I have for you. I've become swept up and away by you and the things you do – the wonderful ways you make me feel. The night is such a beautiful one and the way you are making me feel is the same – let alone the numerous times you've brought me to orgasm already.

Now I can feel it inside you – building up, I can tell you're ready to explode. You cup the back of my head, twining your fingers through my hair; your breathing in my ear becomes labored – deeper. Soon I'll hear your sweet sound of pleasure that always sends goose bumps dashing up and all over my skin.

As I lose myself to you – you lose yourself into me. Opening my eyes, I notice the sky has darkened with pink and reddish shades fading into the background and once again I hear the night sounds, as they were when we arrived. There is nothing like getting fucked in the open with naught around us but nature. You'll never cease to amaze me.

GOOD NIGHT
SWEETHEART

AS I'M SITTING ON the beach, basking in the warm sunshine, the rays feel so good upon my skin. I close my eyes – breath in the scent of the ocean, listening to the waves rolling over and under – the peace of it all relaxes my mind and body. For a while I drift along with my surroundings, opening my eyes to the sights before me.

I begin to slowly rub lotion onto my legs, as I'm doing this I start to daydream about you. Reminiscing of the way you drizzle oil all over me – how your touch stirs the embers deep within, feeling your strong hands spreading my legs apart, your fingers gliding up and down every inch of me – to the tip of my toes. Your grip is firm and feels so nice, taking both of your hands, swirling them around and around my belly. I've been holding my breath and slowly release it with a small moan, arching my back slightly – suddenly I think to myself, you didn't even touch my hottest spot, you rubbed right past my pussy.

But your hands are persistent and they begin to cup my breasts, squeezing gently – pumping the soft tanned flesh of my tits, tweaking my nipples with your fingertips, oh, and the sensations you've ignited inside me! My nerve endings feel so alive with all the attention of every single touch you lay upon me. Teasing me so subtly, seducing my senses to the point where I want to scream out, 'take me – please, take me now!' But I will not do it; I don't want to succumb to it just yet. If I can be patient and let the anticipation build – my explosion in the end will be so worth the wait.

Your beautiful bronzed hands take my arms and stretch them fully out to their sides, you drip more oil onto my tits – taking the excess and spreading it evenly around and out – all the way to my fingertips, intertwining your fingers with mine, our eyes become locked as our hands have and you slowly lay yourself upon my body – never blinking, never unlocking hands, the intensity is so extreme I have to remember to breath. Your lips press against mine and you kiss me with so much passion and want that I feel my heart will surely burst. Time… is standing still.

Enveloping myself with the visions my mind had created; reality brings me out of my deep thoughts. I was in such a daze – I noticed that my body has been covered with lotion, all the while believing that my hands had become yours. I was quiet content, rubbing myself, wrapped up in a daydream of how you can bring such pleasures to me with the simple touch of your hands. Breathing a long deep sigh, wishing sometimes daydreams could be realities. My body is completely relaxed now as if you did just rub me down – looking out along the horizon, it begins to mesmerize me.

As a seabird spreads its wings to take off – I begin my flight, thinking to myself of how I want you so badly now. The need inside has reached its peak – my body yearns to be taken. To be able to fuck you – have your cock inside me, you always seem to be so hard and big for my sweet pussy and oh, how you fuck my ass, the wetness you seem to bring out of me – pure fuckin pleasure – a whole different dimension. I wondered, would I be a lucky girl today and to my surprise, the phone was ringing – calling me back from yet another hot fantasy I was indulging in.

Hearing your voice on the line hits every excited nerve inside my body. The deepness and strength of your tone electrifies me. I begin to tell you how frisky I'm feeling – that I'd love to just throw you down and have my way with you – suck on your cock 'til it's oh so BIG and HARD and just fuck you, have you and take you! The words out of your mouth were the same as mine and you were saying, "Good, keep your thoughts, at least we're on the same horny track because baby, I want to fuck you too." Mentally I prepare myself – thinking of how great it's going to be when you fuck me.

Later that evening, after the sun had gone down, we met at your place – out by the poolside. The lanterns along the pool illuminated the area with a magical glow. It was a perfect, comfortable midsummer night. The scent of the air was heavy with laurel and pine and the stillness among the trees was entrancing.

We sat together on the lounge chair and made some small talk. I noticed that your dick was beginning to protrude from your shorts. My thoughts quickly turned to sucking on you and automatically my hand reaches down to caress your manhood. Oh the feeling of your cock in my hands – so ready and willing. To think that we have sat this close to each other with out any physical contact and your dick has risen to its fullest. You must be really horny, I thought to myself – as much as I am.

Quietly and very gently, I bend over and begin sucking on you; my mouth fills up with your cock. My lips glide up and down continuously, the moisture begins to build inside my mouth as if it had its own orgasm and slowly trickles down the length of your cock. I can only take this for so long because I'm already so wound up from earlier in the day, of wanting to be fucked by you as it was happening now … at this moment.

You reach out to my breasts and begin fondling them; they fit perfectly in the palm of your hands, twirling my nipples with your fingertip and thumb, bringing them quickly to erect little nubs. I've become so entranced in sucking on your cock, feeling your hands upon me – everything around me seems to have disappeared – there is only you and I.

I feel my pussy beginning to moisten, my clit starts to tingle and you seem to be aware of what's going on inside me, as if I were sending you signals. Your one hand remains on my breast as the other reaches down to caress my juicy pussy. Your finger rubs my clit up and down – spreading the wetness all around, then you slip your middle finger into the deepness of my juice and begin to finger-fuck me.

We've got a good foreplay rhythm going on that I'm surprised one of us hasn't given in to just getting fucked yet. I'm still sucking on your cock – feeling the throbbing against the walls of my mouth – massaging your balls – running light strokes of fingernails up and down the inside of your thighs. My saliva is coming out of my mouth sliding down your shaft just as much as the cum is flowing out of my pussy all over your finger.

Out of nowhere but with such ease, you slip your finger into my ass – gently and slowly you push further. You begin to move in and out, in and out and oh my God, I think I'm going to explode, so much is happening at once. I swiftly come up from sucking on you and with a nervous breath, tell you that, "If I don't have your cock inside me soon – I'm going to fuckin' go crazy!"

Attempting to gather ourselves from that intense foreplay, unsteadily I follow you into your bedroom – removing my clothing as we go. Knowing our time is limited; I whisper that, "I'd like you to fuck my ass tonight instead of my pussy." Leaning towards me as you whisper in your husky voice, "With pleasure, my hot -n- horny juicy, dripping, little box."

I lay down on the floor and you kneel in front of me grabbing a handful of your cock – stroking your beautiful erection. "Please fuck me – you are making me so off the wall horny, I can't take another minute." Inserting a finger into my ass, your eyes seek out mine, my ass is so wet and open – looking back at you with acknowledgement, there's no need for ease and gentleness – I'm totally ready for you. Teasing my ass a little with your finger, the liquid slides down my crack – sucking on my nipples here and there; my body is absolutely going to ignite and it is screaming inside. "Please fuck my ass – I want your dick inside me – I need to feel that penetration."

Lying on top of me, smoothly slipping your hard cock into my wet ass, man – you are so big, the rush of feeling flutters through my entire body, having you fully inside me, finally, is beyond comprehension but everything I asked for. What a feeling – what a friggin rush. Fucking my ass this way gets me so hot and bothered – I knew I was ready for it. You fuck my ass so good – your cock moves in and out and in and out, sometimes slowly and gently and then you'll be moving faster and faster – bringing me to orgasm with every changing speed.

I pick up my legs and spread them open – which brings your cock deeper inside of me. Bending your head down you suck on my nipples giving each a little attention. You've awakened every possible nerve inside my body – from head to toe and their standing on end, waiting for the next rush. Reaching down to my clit, I rub it with each penetrating stroke as you give my ass. I begin to rub myself faster and with more urgency, as your dick keeps pulsating inside of me.

Along with your sucking on my nipples, kissing me passionately hard, and just fucking my ass, I relax myself so that I can feel every movement – closing my eyes and yielding to the tornado of emotions swirling throughout my being. You have created this and I'm holding on to whatever thing my hands can reach, my feet grasping to land on anything – something sturdy.

"Oh yeah – you are so fucking good; you fuck my ass so good. Don't stop, please don't stop, I'm so wet, my ass is coming so good, you make me so fucking crazy." The orgasms keep swirling through me, higher and higher – twisting and turning. I'm so wrapped up in how you're fucking me – the rush keeps building and burning. I feel as though our bodies have become one, entangled in our liaison, you're giving me exactly what I wanted.

To have you fuck my ass – needing you in the place that is supposed to be forbidden. I believe I'm beginning to go numb – my breathing is uneven – I'm drifting to the unknown, where everything that I'm feeling has begun to collide and crash – molding itself into one – the eruption is inevitable.

My moans become louder, my words more distinct, "Fuck me, oh yeah, please don't stop, right there – stay right there, ooohh

ooh, fuck me ... fuck me ... fuck me!" I breath in the deepest
breath and for a moment ... nothing ... stillness ... and in one
exhale ... I let it all go with a scream so full of release that you've
gotten tangled in my web and have begun your own crossing.

You keep fucking me with such determination until you
bring yourself to the edge – I can see it in your eyes, piercing
into mine – your face has it written all over, with every drop
of sweat, every ounce of energy – you give way to a roar that
is like a lions, who has triumphed. To watch you build up and
explode is like nothing I've ever seen before. We collapse and fall
together – remembering that there is a world out there.

YOU ARE THE BEST

WHEN WE SPOKE ON the phone that morning, I asked, "What would you like me to bring?" Your answer was – the basic essentials and just yourself. So, I took your words to heart and showed up only with baby oil and myself. "Did you take me literally," you asked? "Of course I did – we had all the playtime we needed yesterday. Today is fully straightforward, fuck me sex."

I just couldn't wait to be with you again so I immediately began to undress. You rinsed yourself in the shower, came over to the bed, drinking in the sight of my naked – sprawled out body, beckoning you to me. You laid your beautiful golden body over mine.

My fingers skimmed over your muscular back, hands grabbing at your ass and working their way to trace the length of your arms. "MMM... what a gorgeous man you are, every inch of you, in every aspect of the word man." Your skin so smooth, perfect to the touch, fills up my senses. Your lips brush against my sensitive nipples and suckle each one – your tongue swirls around the erectness 'til they become perfect little peaks of hardened skin. Your mouth consumes my tit as your tongue keeps its dance – round and round my nipple. You seem to be enjoying the time you take on each mound of flesh.

I've completely lost track of sanity, except for the creeping sensation you are beginning to create inside of me. I hear your whispered words of such beautiful, soft, perfect titties – moaning in response to your voice, my eyes close and my hands continue

142

their travels over your lean body. Each time you send me reeling, I grab a part of your ass cheek and firmly knead it, while my other hand holds onto your waist – holding onto you any way I can. My legs intertwine with yours and I have you in a strong embrace. My world has become timeless – my breath indrawn, sexually I have risen … peaked … fallen and exhaled. You seduce me so magically; I feel I'm in a trance.

Releasing your hold on me just a bit, my eyes flip open and I stare deep into the blue of yours. Your arm, the length of my body, stretches downward and your hand cups my ass and it fits perfectly in the palm of your strong hand. Your eyes – so penetrating, I see and feel the lust in them. My fingers glide through the strands of your hair, playfully tugging at the ends, even your hair – so soft and golden, sets my heart to a beat of it's own.

Your lips find mine with a kiss so light, but yet … so strong – reverberating all the passion inside you into me. Your tongue dances with mine, tracing the outline of my lips and nibbling with your teeth, then your tongue licks me across my bottom lip, skimming over my upper lip. Moisture from your mouth seeps into mine as though you had an orgasm. Feeling your kisses and the teasing of your tongue, delivers the thoughts visually of you sucking and teasing on my pussy – having you between my legs, even though you are all over my face and my mouth begins to bring forth its own wetness – you've made my mouth cum. "Unbelievable" – I say, you are so amazing and I am so horny for you and all that you have to offer.

We've become so engrossed and tangled up with each other that we can feel our blood flowing like a mad river – raging throughout its course, twisting – turning – and rushing forward to its final destination. I'm feeling so fucking combustible that somehow you always seem to sense my level of sexual anxiety – from head to toe. My core is on its last nerve-ending and your voice … sweet talking in my ear, tells me that it's okay, it's alright to cum as much as I do – you're a horny little cunt, that's all.

As you slide your hand over my face and place butterfly kisses all over me – I feel I've been strummed like a smooth instrument. Inching your way down, caressing each pink – hardened, oh so very sensitive nipple, prolonging your stay just to see me squirm and looking up at me with that mischievous, boyish little grin – there's only one place your headed and I let out a sigh because I know … I know.

Your powerful hands slide under my ass and you settle yourself in, to suck my pussy! All that sweet juicy cum running out of my pussy, even though your dick never entered me, is because of how you loved my body and kissed me so – that you sent me to the edge, so many times – but never took me over. You just chased and teased me, time and time again, pushing me closer – but always pulling me back to reality by your ever-changing ways. You fuck me, even though you didn't really fuck me!

Bubbling with pleasure, I tell you how amazing I think you are. Of course – deep down – I know and you know, that it isn't over and we're both not fulfilled until your cock is in my cunt. Chasing my thoughts away, I place a pillow under my head – wrap my arms behind it and watch your beautiful blond head, tilt and turn, swaying to and fro. Your mouth nuzzles my pussy, your eyes turn up towards mine and your hands reach out to my belly, gently pressing in or pushing upwards, making my insides squeeze and quiver. Mmm … I let out a wonderful sigh – your tongue is so very naughty. You look so damn good between my legs – pure delight … and those startling blue eyes piercing straight through into mine … into the depths of my soul.

Your mouth devours my cunt, licking at the juices – weaving your tongue, making figure eights, passing over my clit – crossing over my hole. Oh man, what a fucking rush – you're making me crazy and I'm not going to be able to control my intensifying orgasmic waves. You've turned the nozzle on and from this point – until you stop sucking on my pussy, I'll continually keep cumming for you – I'll surrender my sweet juices unto you.

Closing my eyes, I concentrate on you, the way you feel on my cunt – every lick – every move, the heat from your tongue, even your breath against my pussy lips. I can feel it all – "Oh God – you're making me nuts." I can't stop the honey from dripping, you suck on me so good, "Oh Yeah – that's it – lick it, suck it – Oh lick it baby, don't stop, that's purrfect!" I can tell you've lost it too because I'm watching you and you are so intent on what you're doing, your eyes are closed and your mouth is working it's magic. You look so content, as a child peacefully sucking its thumb. But you are not a child – and this is no thumb you're sucking. Gazing at you for a while seems to have mesmerized me again.

Slowly I begin to fondle my tits – every now and again I tug at my nipples. I reach down to pull up on the top of my pussy and when my clit escapes your mouth – your tongue darts out to flick at it and your teeth recaptures it, ohhh … what a spasm – you just sent the shivers down my backbone. When I play with my nipples and you've got a hold of my clit – it all feels so connected – like a cable of electricity surging from one point to the next; back and forth, up and down – working me into another orgasmic frenzy.

Before I can even begin to think straight or regain consciousness, you've found a way to stay attached to my hot pussy, but have positioned yourself on your knees, near my head so that now I have the ability to suck on your cock. Oh sweet heaven, I'm thinking to myself. Without hesitation to please you, as you are pleasing me – so fucking good, I take a hold of your already hard – throbbing shaft and begin licking it, up and down and all around. You are my favorite lollipop – always hard, sweet to the taste and you never let me down. Your manhood is so fine looking and so big; my mouth drools to suck on it.

Again you seem to sense my want and need – you understand my body language so well and position yourself just right and in you go; my mouth takes a hold of your cock. Oh yeah … this is blissful – orally connected to each other and giving pleasure to one another!

Now we're lying on our sides and your tongue has slowed its dance around my wet, horny cunt, but I understand the meaning, you want to savor and concentrate on this cock sucking that you are getting. Pleasuring you with a little bit of a head job, in and out – up and down and nudging my tongue into the slit of your top hat, teasing and swirling – round and round your rim. With one downward motion I take all of you inside and feel the thickness of your cock consuming my mouth.

Shivers run through my body as I hear your words breathed upon my pussy – "You sure can suck some good cock – my sweet juicy box." On the way up from the bottom of your shaft, I spread my tongue flat and lick you back and forth, slowly rising up to greet the head of your cock. Your rich and seductive voice fills my senses and transports me to seventh heaven – I am so lost again and nothing matters but sucking on your pulsating cock.

Gently tugging at the hair on your balls, tenderly cupping them in my hand as I wrap my other hand around your massive hardness, going into over-drive, my body is revving – my mind is screaming and my pussy is so fucking HOT. I feel the explosion … rising and taking control. With a receiving mouth you're there, sucking and drinking in my juices – swirling my cream all over my cunt. Letting go of your dick, I beg you to suck me, "Please" … breathlessly pleading, "Suck my pussy – Oh baby – please lick my cunt, lick me all over, don't stop – you're going to make me cum AGAIN … ohhh shit – I'm going to … oooo – here it comes, Oh fuck, you fucking suck my pussy sooo damn good!"

All of a sudden my world seems to be unsteady as you lift my hips slightly in the air, off the bed, so my pussy meets your face, you're actually cradling me – suspending me half way up. In a ragged breath I tell you that I feel like play-dough, my bones and limbs are numb, I have no control – what ounce I do have left is not worth anything. I am your toy – mold and shape me any way you want. I cannot believe you're still going at it, sucking my pussy and drinking in the delights. Feeling quite subdued, I softly ask, "Am I the sweetest you've ever had?" and I hear the sound of your muffled enjoyment chiming in with my escaping moans.

I've hit my highest point, reaching out for anything, sparks igniting inside – shooting skyward and cascading all about. My voice sounds as if I'm partly crying – "You suck me so very well, such a good pussy licker, oh – such a lucky little girl I am, good … hot … juicy … orgasmic pussy! You love sucking your little cunt, don't you, you know I'm yours – I belong to you."

Incoherently – conscious and unconsciously words spill from my lips, my eyelids twitch, my body begins to tremble and my every last nerve shoots straight to my heart – making it thump madly – as full blown goose-bumps sweep across my being and I scream it all out, every rush that expanded inside, all the bubbles begin bursting. The eternity of your pussy pleasuring has come to an end and my emotions are like a slinky, flip – down … flop – down … flip-flop, back down … to earth.

Slowly you bring my legs back to the bed, trying to catch my breath, I begin stretching my legs straight out – reaching my arms to the ceiling, then stretching my body out from head to toe. I am so relaxed, so melted – I feel like a Cheshire cat, you've made my pussy purr. You are amazing – what bliss could be better!

Face to face, your eyes focused on mine – your mouth nestles close, as our lips brush each other's, you so softly and tenderly kiss me, giving me a little taste of my own sweet juice. Our kiss becomes frantic, your mouth closes hard on mine – harsh but gentle – you've woven a web all around my body, I'm caught – entrapped by your seducing power. Our bodies are attached in every way possible, in such a strong embrace that will not be broken.

Moving sensually inside me, you plunge deep down; our journey begins with only one destination. Stroke after pulsating stroke your pace grows faster, you have me held in your vice grip arms, feeling every inch of my hot cunt, enveloped perfectly around your hard cock, pushing further – driving deeper, with all that you've got. My voice is raspy and mixed with burning 'Fuck Me' desire. "Yeah, that's it baby, you fuck your pussy so good, Oh yeah – come on, give that pussy a good fucking, give me what you got – I want it all, I want you deeper," and like a spell has been cast upon you, you push your cock down, deeper – drilling it home, to the core of my existence.

Listening to your voice telling me not to stop talking, you want to hear about the fucking that I'm getting, about the long pussy sucking you gave me – remember it all and speak to me of it, how you took pleasure in every single lick of it. The words spew forth from my mouth and I feel your body tense and clasp mine more tightly and now I know you are at the edge and Oh baby – I'm going to help push you over!

"Come on you beautiful fucked up man – fuck my pussy, give it – give it to me – I want it – I want it so bad! I want to feel you explode inside me – feel you shudder against my body. I want you to scream and release every bit of your orgasm into your sweet ... hot ... waiting juice box. Give your cunt the fucking it deserves, you rule my cunt – it's yours – you are the only one who can fuck it the way you do – fuck me, fuck me, Oh please, please ... fuck my pussy ... come for me, come inside my squeeze box – that's right, Oh yeah, that's it."

Feeling your body through the palms of my hands, as if you were sending me signals, I know you are almost there, so ready to spill into me – your breathing is harsh and labored, your burning blue eyes send me shooting sparks of sexual combustion. The expression on your face with every crinkled line tells me how you're going to ignite – you are not breathing, your eyes are bulging, your face is turning red and I'm in a transfixed state just watching the display of you. I'm holding my breath as well and you exhale the burst of orgasmic energy. Your scream – tantalizing, but sounding tormented, is more of a song to my ears than any other tune I've ever heard.

Shaking and trembling until you unwind and return back to me with full comprehension, I stare up at you in wonderment. Lying on top of me, you cradle me in your arms with whatever strength you have left, your deep ragged breathing becomes more steady and you whisper into my left ear ... "You are such a sweet, sweet piece of ass ... my horny, lucky, little cunt ... "

ONLY THE
BEGINNING

WALKING INTO THE ROOM, I didn't expect it to look the way it did – the bed was circular with tree branches coming out of the wall, going in all different directions; my eyebrows raised and I thought nasty thoughts of … just hanging around. The tub was enclosed by a waterfall – surrounded by rocks, foliage and places to comfortably sit around the edges, again my mind wandered over it with delight. I began to feel the rush from the tip of my toes to the top of the hairs on my head, ooh yeah; as the sensations coursed through me; it made me all tingly inside.

Reaching out towards you and grabbing your body, I begin to undo your belt – slipping my fingers through your button fly, kissing your straight and narrow – hot lips, as I inch your jeans down below your hips – to your ankles, just enough to keep you trapped. Placing my thumbs in your waistband, pulling open towards me to release that nice big cock and he wants out – oh so badly – I work your underwear down just enough to let him go.

Wrapping my hands around your thighs – kneeling to the floor in submissiveness, I drop my head to your commanding cock and into my wanting mouth you slide. Your head is so smooth going in, running my tongue around your rim, through your slit; it's enough to almost fill my mouth. My eyes drifting shut, I begin to lose myself and your cock sucking takes on a life of its own.

Your hips have begun to move to my pace – you jut yourself into me quickly, hands guiding my head with slight pressure, teasing me you take it away just as fast as you gave it. I look straight up at you, eyes gleaming and nip down on you gently. I hear you saying that, "I'm a hot, juicy little cunt and you know that my pussy wants it bad and needs it good." Smiling... I wink up at you.

Then I proceed to take your bulging hard cock as deep and far as it'll go, reaching in between your legs to pump your balls with the tips of my fingers; petting them up and down, placing a finger straight against your rigid shaft as my mouth glides over your pulsating beautiful cock. Mmm... I lose myself so easily to this wonderful connection, thinking that this could be my pussy you're sliding in and out of, my juice box begins flowing and I'm realizing how wet I've become.

Abruptly my world goes crooked, your arms – hands, are grasping at me – finding what ever you can reach, dipping and scooping inside my shirt, to my bra, onto my round perky tits. Guessing this is some kind of release for you, because if I'm sucking – you need to be touching. I keep my mouth wrapped around you and your hand covers my titty; pumping at my flesh, twirling my erect nipples between your thumb and finger.

I can no longer bear this swirl of intoxicating rushes. So I pull away from your hardness – sit back and begin to undress. I look up to see that you have stripped all your clothes off and are waiting naked – your golden body; sprawled out on the bed, beckoning me... to you. My pussy is so ready and willing – I want it badly – I need you inside me, like NOW!

Lying on my back, you dive into my hot center of wetness – "Oh, you are so bad, you can't just fuck me and give it to me, you need to tease me and make me cum a little more." After drooling all over your cock, you should have known how often I came and now, here you are – deliciously sucking up my sweetness. Your mouth covers my pussy and you devour me so well – I hear your moans, like you're eating the best you've ever tasted – "Oh yeah, you suck me so good, I am so wet, my pus can't help but overflow for you – you are so sweet to my 'lil pussy."

I lay my head down and take all that you give, every stroke of your tongue – I feel, every suckle on my clit – shoots instantly through me, up to my nipples and oooo – I have to rub my titties to calm my senses down, because I feel as though I'm going to burst!

After you've had your fill of my sweet cum, you begin to trail yourself upwards, dribbling out a line of juice along the way, directly to my mouth, your hands capture my face – you take a firm hold of my head and kiss me as if our lips have never met – with a soft, but savage I'm going to rule you kiss. Seeping out what's left of my sweetness into my mouth, receiving it gladly – your eyes pierce into mine as the exchange takes place.

Grabbing for your ass with one hand and holding onto your back with my other arm – I clamp down on you, holding you in a vice grip and kissing you back with fervor, letting you know that you own me – you have me, you can take me anytime – "Please," I whisper in your ear, "Please fuck me – I can't take this waiting any longer – give it to me … please!"

You plunge into the depths of my wantonness, arching a little, receiving you – pushing my head backwards, exposing my neck to you – which you take for more pleasure and drop kisses along my throat. I let out a long awaited sigh … mmm – ahhh, then I wrap both my arms around your broad back, raise my hips to your pounding and ride the cascading waves of satisfaction that spill over me.

Finally, you're fucking me, I'm in my glory and man … this is what I've been waiting for – been waiting to collide with you. You build me up and build me up to this moment, until I feel like a firecracker with my fuse lit. Your big cock fucks my juicy little pussy and there isn't anything better than feeling the connection of our bodies – holding on to each other so tightly until we reach our highest point. The firecrackers … POP … POP … POP, POP, POP and I scream out into the air, releasing the explosion inside.

I turn my attention to you – your eyes are glazed, your lips move but no words are spoken – your breathing has become labored, I know you're almost there. I begin speaking to you – "Give it to me, fuck my pussy, give it to me please ... my pussy is yours – yours to fuck, suck and play with, I belong to you – I'm your little horny pussy, such a hot juicy cunt who loves getting fucked by your big ... hard ... cock," and all of a sudden it happens so quickly – you explode with such a gust of emotion, like a roar from a lion – it just spills out from inside you. It totally blows me away, every time you let go – it's always fascinating to watch – your release is so driven, so damn intense, I'm in total awe.

You collapse onto me, your breathing has slowed, but I feel your heart racing on my chest and the sweat trickles off of you, down on to me and trickles along my sides. I stroke my palms across your body, down your back and hush your breathing until it returns to normal and wipe away the dampness from you. We intertwine ourselves and touch each other calmly as we regain our sense of self.

After some time of lazing around, we venture into the tub – your husky laugh fills the room as you speak, "Now that the serious stuff is out of the way, it's playtime!" Laughing with you, I agree shyly. We sink down into the warmth that bubbles all around our bodies. I reach for the soap, as you suspiciously pour bubble bath into the water and look at me with a sheepish, sly grin. I continue to soap and massage your shoulders and neck, down your arms – up to your chest, lathering you until my hands glide from one side to the other. Such a manly body to delight my hands with – as I get into what I'm doing, your hand seeks out my pussy and you start pulling at my clit.

Wriggling away from you my tits pop up and you stick your tongue out to graze over my nipple – "Oh ... you are so naughty," but I push my tits more into your face and pull you closer to me. "Now who's the bad one," you ask? Your mouth encloses over my taut nipple and you begin sucking – licking, as your finger slides into my hole. Your thumb nudges at my clit, I'm beginning to feel intoxication seep through my veins – I'm totally relaxed and just go with it.

Reaching into the water, I gently rub your hard cock,

grasping onto it as it fills up my tiny hand – everything feels so good, it's all making me want more and as usual you know what buttons to push and how far to push, you bring me to a certain height – just enough to go over the edge, but then … you retreat. I tell you that you're such a tease and in reply – you tell me to suck your cock, as you inch yourself up onto the side, "I've got something you can tease."

Happy to oblige, I place my hands on either side of your thighs, with an open mouth, I sink down – inch by inch – onto your jutting cock. Sucking up and down as you pull me a little higher up, out of the water until I'm kneeling. Your strong hand flutters down my spine, grabbing a hold of my ass – you press into the flesh of my cheek. I wrap a hand around your shaft and hold your balls in my other hand, as I connect the dots and join in the rhythm of all that's happening. Your finger twirls around the opening of my asshole – pleasing and teasing, exciting me until it goes up to my pussy hole, back and forth you begin to rub and once again … all is lost but the motion of our playfulness. Inching closer and bringing myself up because I want more of your finger in my asshole – you follow where I'm going and slide a finger slowly inside. I get such a rush from the entrance and knowing that this is only the beginning of so much more to come, I release your cock from my mouth and hold it – stroke it and massage your pulsating flesh, you get so big just from playing with me.

Your mouth seeks mine, your tongue darts out across my lips – you nip at me as I lick your lips and suckle them. We exchange such passion in our kiss that I become so high from it, as our tongues do a tango of their own. I brush my lips over your face and gently bite into your shoulder, only to return to your roaming mouth – Oh the things that turn me on about you.

Out of body and just floating with the current of sensations, I find myself out of the water and sitting on the edge of the tub, next to you. Without missing a beat, you tell me to relax and I think, well, that's kind of strange, because it doesn't get any better than this and if I relax any more I'll turn into butter … melted butter.

All of a sudden though, I realize that there is more than one finger delighting my asshole, you lower your head to suck on my nipple as I position myself for better comfort, kneeling on the edge of the tub. I hear you whisper softly – sweetly, "Shh... I'm going to take you higher then you've ever been." The energy that surges through me is unexplainable, you never cease to amaze me and I have no idea what I'm in for – my eyes dreamily begin to close to my surroundings.

Taking it all in and receiving everything you offer me – with an open mind and body – I feel as though I'm slipping into the unknown, but because I'm with you, I feel safe on this untraveled path. Lowering my head, I give into the weakness, but feeling other senses... stretching – wavering, leaping over unsteady ground. My insides tighten and shake all over, sucking in my breath, your pace started out slow but has rapidly progressed – I can't help it but I want more, my need for pleasure is like some crazy dream with no relation to reality.

A confusion of sensations enclose me – every inch of my being, you kiss my mouth – my cheeks – my eyes, nose and forehead and than take my lips again until the shadows find themselves inside of my world. Unable to think, drifting further into the fog – dimming reason to disorder, feeling as if I've been sent to drift and drowning deep – I realize that what ever it is you are doing has made me flush myself all over your hand! The liquid poured out of me like an afternoon pop-up rain shower – it took me by surprise as it became all so real.

My eyes searched – my mind questioned until I focused on you and in the faint light, your sky blue eyes gave me reassurance. I thought you had stopped, you only just slowed down and I began breathing in long gusts as the rip current passed through me again – my mouth opened and shut... but no words came out, the trickle of warmth gathered in a puddle under my feet and I wrapped myself around your body and held on for the rest of the journey.

Clasping you tightly – not a word was spoken between us,

just the sound of our breathing – letting me feel the force of this surprising... unbelievable experience; until my breathing settled to a rational pace – the levels in the quick shift of mind and emotion were like a blast of wind that came and vanished. I was in such awe – my complete total being was numb – you touched me in such a way that bewildered my mind and left me spellbound. I looked into your smiling eyes and kissed you – bringing you into me, asking quietly because I had to know – "Did that really happen!"

Teasingly you asked if I'd like to feel it again, my eyes opened wide with curiosity, and drawing back a bit, I declined timidly. Wandering to myself is it even possible... could it actually... could I actually do it again?

You pulled me close and cradled me until my breathing settled to a normal beat, reassuring me with butterfly kisses that all was well while I held onto you as if you were my life raft.

Printed in the United States
By Bookmasters